Courage Under Fire

Edited by Tyree Campbell

Courage Under Fire
March 2024
Edited by Tyree Campbell

All rights reserved. No part of this book may be reproduced or transmitted in any form or by any means, electronic or mechanical, including photocopying or recording or by any information storage and retrieval systems, without expressed written consent of the authors and/or artists.

Courage Under Fire is a work of fiction. Names, characters, places, and incidents are products of the authors' imaginations. Any resemblance to actual events or persons, living or dead, is entirely coincidental.

Story and illustration copyrights owned by the respective authors.

Cover art "The 7:15 Adventure" by Laura Givens
Cover design by Laura Givens

First Printing March 2024
Hiraeth Publishing
http://hiraethsffh.com/
@HiraethPublish1

Visit http://hiraethsffh.com/ for online science fiction, fantasy, horror, scifaiku, and more. Also visit the Hiraeth Publishing bookstore for paperbacks, magazines, anthologies, and chapbooks. Support the small, independent press…

Contents

Short Stories

7	Still Fighting by Jasmine Grace
21	Jamais Vu by Maureen Mancini Amaturo
31	Fearfully and Wonderfully Made by Veronica Leigh
47	A Nice Girl Like You by Tyree Campbell
76	The Free Zone by Barbara Candiotti
84	How I Saved the World and Got Grounded for Six Months by James Rumpel

Poems

20	Bad Vibes by Debby Feo
20	Ghost Planet by Randall Andrews
46	Spaced Out by Debby Feo
97	Who's Who?

Illustration

30	Confronting the Demon by Sandy DeLuca

Iuliae: Past Tense
By Tyree Campbell

Two sisters of the Iulius Family have run away from the restrictions and rules of their settlement on a remote world, and embark on a journey of discovery, to learn what to do with their new-found freedom. Along the way, they become smugglers, and opponents of human trafficking, and become fugitives from the law and from the corporations.

Iulia Sexta, the younger of the two sisters, is suffering from an identity crisis. Is it gender dysphoria? Was she supposed to be a man? Is that why she likes girls? Or is a ghost from one of her previous lives now trying to haunt his way back into the living by taking over her body and mind?

With both the past and the present pursuing them, Iulia Tertia and Iulia Sexta find their future under constant attack. Doing the right thing is not only difficult at best, but may well result in their deaths. What to do? One thing at a time…

https://www.hiraethsffh.com/product-page/iuliae-past-tense-by-tyree-campbell

A Little Help, Please

In the world of the small indie press we fight a never-ending battle for attention to our work, as writers and in publishing. Here's an example: big publishers [you know who they are] have gobs of $$$ that they can devote to advertising and marketing. Here at Hiraeth Publishing, our advertising budget consists of the deposits for whatever soda bottles and aluminum cans we can find alongside the highways. Anti-littering laws make our task even more difficult . . . ☺

That's where YOU come in. YOU are our best promoter. YOU are the one who can tell others about us. Just send 'em to our website, tell them about our store. That's all. Just that.

Of course, we don't mind if you talk us up. We're pretty good, you know. We have some award-winning and award-nominated writers and artists, plus other voices well-deserving to be heard [not everyone wins awards, right?] but our publications are read-worthy nevertheless.

That number once again is:

www.hiraethsffh.com

Friend us on Facebook at Hiraeth Publishing
Follow us on Twitter at @HiraethPublish1

Still Fighting
Jasmine Grace

Blood dripped down my arm as I raised my sword in the air. I rotated in the center of the arena, looking up at the spectators. A crowd of several thousand. There were more today than the last fight. One by one, then in small groups, then by the hundreds, they stood and cheered.
Even as the drones above buzzed overhead, snapping pictures and videos of every soul that dared show such defiance to the Queen, more people rose to their feet.

Now I faced the Queen herself. She didn't sit with her citizens on the rough stone benches surrounding the circular arena. She sat on a vintage velvet couch in a box separated from the commoners by graceful wrought iron bars and her armed guards, human and droid.

The guard nearest to her leaned in close as she muttered orders to him. He relayed the message to his radio, and signaled to the drones above. Soldiers descended on the crowds, forcing the people to quiet down and take their seats.

None of them were supposed to be cheering for the prisoner who was not supposed to be alive.

The Queen looked at me in disgust.

I smiled at her, and stuck my sword into the dirt floor of the arena, burying it halfway up the blade. Despite the guards, the crowd roared.

Slim steel gates slid open behind me. Guards entered the arena. A squad pulled me back through the gates while the rest cleared the bodies from the arena.

I was led out of the arena into the tunnels below. These were carved of the same rough stone as the rest of the arena. An ancient, crude material. Everything else in the city was polished glass and glittering steel and neon lights. But this place was ancient, primitive. Just like the fights that took place in the arena above.

Soon we reached the prisons. They had been full when I first arrived, occupied by fellow criminals and opponents of the Queen. They were still packed, but largely with new prisoners. The daily fights to the death ensured no one survived here very long.

I expected to be thrown back in my cell, where I would wait for the next fight rigged against me, but the guards pushed me forward, and we continued to a sort of a kennel beneath the prisons. We passed lions, bears, and boars, among other creatures. These were the animals the Queen added to the fights when she wanted to make things more interesting.

The guards threw me into a cell that held only a pile of hay and a bucket of water. My previous cell had at least held a proper bed.

Most of the guards left then, but one, a younger boy, stayed to lock the door behind me.

"You're pissing off the Queen," he hissed.

I laughed. Couldn't help it. Any idiot could tell she wasn't happy. "Any other news?"

He frantically put his fingers to his lips. There were no cameras down here in these ancient tunnels, as the Queen didn't want any record of her treatment of prisoners. But in this city the walls had ears, maybe even down here.

He didn't want anyone to know he'd tried to give a warning to a prisoner.

I used the bars to pull myself to a standing position, towering over him. I was unnaturally tall for a woman, or so I had been told.

He looked up at me. "The longer you survive here, the grislier your end will be. She wants you to suffer. She wants to send you to the Labs."

I would rather die than end up in the Labs. That was where the Queen's most heartless scientists experimented on all variety of creatures, combining the strongest parts of animals into even stronger hybrids. Soldiers and mercenaries of the Queen.

The process of having one's mind and body merged with another was hellish, and a frightening percentage of those who entered the Labs died on some Gods-forsaken operating table. Those who survived lost all of their freedom. Not only were they prisoners for life, they had to share a mind and body with another creature.

But this boy didn't get to see my fear. I just shrugged. "No matter what, this doesn't end well for me. The least I can do is stir things up a little before then." My voice was barely a whisper. He had good intentions, if nothing else.

He nodded, looking down at the dirt on the floor.

"That's noble," he said. "I wish you luck, if that means anything."

I snorted. "Luck means nothing. However, an open lock would mean everything."

He kicked at the dirty floor. "If I did that, she'd kill me, then I'd be replaced. You'd piss her off even more, then you'd die too. In the Labs or the arena. It would mean nothing."

I could hear Fioni in my head, telling me that any of us can make a difference, that even the cogs in a machine are noticed when they stop turning.

Then I could hear Bry, saying individuals amount to nothing, no matter what we did. That cogs are meaningless, replaceable. Only organizations, collections of individual cogs working as one, can create change.

The young guard shook his head, turned, and left. But I barely noticed. I was drowning in memories.

I was back in the sewers with Fioni. That was where Rebels dwelled: the labyrinths beneath cities, those places which held more places to hide than anyone bothered to pay attention to. Most are afraid of the darkness. But we knew the darkness kept us safe, and that it was one of the only places in the city without droids on patrol or cameras watching our every move.

That day, though, the sewers had become a trap, not a refuge.

Earlier in the morning, one of the droids had followed Bry to the entrance we used. There were droids in the tunnels, hunting us down, slowly encircling us.

The rebel leaders knew we would have to leave.

Never again would we be able to hide beneath the cities. We would have to flee to the mountains, the wilderness beyond civilization.

Fioni sat beside me, just around the corner from the rebel leaders. We couldn't see them around the corner, but we were close enough to hear every word as they debated our method of escape.

The problem was going to be keeping those tunnels open when the drones inevitably detected the mass exit.

"We could rig the tunnel with traps," someone suggested.

"What kind of trap does a robot fall for?" Bry snapped.

"We could rig them to blow. We have plenty of explosives, and we could fashion a timer easily enough."

"Oh sure, and make the whole city cave in on itself. Any blast big enough to block the tunnels would risk the city above. We can't gamble that many innocent lives," Bry said, beginning to pace. I knew it was him; I knew the rhythm of his footsteps.

"There are plenty of traps that could snare a machine. But those are the types of traps that need a person to stay behind and trigger," someone else suggested.

An uneasy silence settled upon the meeting.

"There are no motion sensors we could set to detect them when they come?" someone else asked.

"No, the droids can detect things like that," Bry said. "Why can't we leave someone to trigger the traps?"

No one dared answer that question. Rebels were closer than family. We never left anyone behind. Not in battle, not on missions, not ever.

I could practically hear Bry roll his eyes. "Come on, just one person. One person to save all of the rest of us?"

It was so quiet we could hear the rats running in the shadows.

"That Fioni is always babbling about how much individuals can make a difference. How about her? Enabling the escape of all rebel forces would certainly be a difference."

I looked to Fioni sitting beside me. Even in the

shadows, her face grew red and angry.

She stood, and stepped around the corner. Several of them started, not expecting Fioni to appear so suddenly.

"If you want to leave someone behind so badly, why don't we leave you?"

"My mind for strategy is unmatched," Bry replied. "No one can replace me, and you know it. If I stay behind, who will plot the next raid or mission?"

He was right. We needed him for the survival of our goal. He wasn't just a cog in the rebel machine, he was the circuit board that ensured the rest of the cogs turned correctly.

"I'll stay," I heard myself saying.

Silence again filled the room.

I waited for Bry to protest. Just that morning, he'd woken me from my cot with a kiss on the forehead, and a sweet bun he'd stolen from the city above. He'd told me he loved me, and we dreamed for a moment about the future we would create for ourselves.

But then he remained silent. It was Fioni that told me no, I couldn't stay. Who told me she needed me, that I couldn't leave her.

In the end, Bry's silent approval had been louder than her increasingly desperate insistence that I must go with the others.

The memories faded, receding like the tide. Then I was alone, with the bulls and panthers in the two neighboring cells. Although the creatures here growled or bared teeth at me, I knew we were all the same. We were all prisoners.

Of all those I'd fought here, none of them had been my enemies. But I wanted to show the Queen that she couldn't rid herself of me so easily. My body and my will to survive were strongest, so I had won all three of my fights.

I had killed human prisoners, laughing hyenas, and today, wolves. I wished I remembered how to pray, so I could beg mercy for their souls. Maybe I would also pray for the safety of my family. The Rebels. I would ask that Bry had the chance to carry on our work. And that Fioni could forgive me for leaving her.

But I hadn't prayed since I was a child, and I had since forgotten how. I had given up faith long ago, preferring to take matters into my own hands rather than leaving them to a mysterious deity. The Gods just never seemed to have enough miracles to go around.

I curled up in the hay, and fell asleep almost immediately. My dreams were of Fioni, whom I missed so dearly, and Bry, the reason I was here.

Most prisoners of the Queen were unlucky folks who attracted the wrong kind of attention or were in the wrong place at the wrong time. But I was guilty of everything I was accused of. And plenty of other things no one had noticed yet.

Of course, none of the things I was accused of I had done alone. The Queen knew that, but she hoped if she could pin all hopes of rebellion on me, then kill me, any thoughts of rebellion would perish. She hoped to show her audience how futile resistance truly was.

But so far, she had only made me famous. Even though no sane citizen liked to witness the barbaric fights of the arena, people had begun to come willingly to my fights.

Fioni's voice echoed in my head.

"Anyone could make a difference in this world. You should stay with the Rebels. We'd be better off throwing Bry to the guards, and leading the rebellion ourselves."

But I had 'gotten caught' by the guards the next day, defending our stronghold. They had known many Rebels had escaped, but, with me, they at least had a scapegoat for their Queen.

Bry, for all his faults, had an excellent mind for strategy. The rebellion would never survive without him. After my eventual death here, I would fade away, one prisoner among many. The rebellion would outlive me.

The Queen and her soldiers haunted my dreams as I slept in my cell. Her human soldiers were even worse than the droids. The droids had no emotions, no capacity for sympathy, no understanding of the pain they caused. The humans did. And somehow, they were crueler than their mechanical counterparts. I was woken by one of them in the morning. It was the boy from the night before.

The one who had tried to warn me.

I sat up, noting the way he kept looking over his shoulder and the piece of paper he had shoved in his belt, beside his radio.

"This... um, you should see this," he said, handing me the paper through the bars.

It was a news piece. The front page was a blown-up image of the dirt floor of the arena, splattered with blood. 'Still Fighting,' read the title.

It was about me. My fights. My victories. My survival.

"I know all this," I said. I was well aware of each and every match I had won, every life I had taken to preserve my own.

"Look at the last section."

I skipped to the bottom of the page. It talked about the increasing cruelty of who I had been forced to fight. How badly the Queen wanted me gone. How, logically, I should be dead, but I had defied everything, and I was still fighting.

It even dared to imply that the Queen didn't have the courage to kill me herself. That she preferred to make her prisoners, human, and animal, do the dirty work for her.

I handed the paper back to him. "Even if everyone in the city reads this, no one wants to join me in the spotlight of the Queen's rage. It means nothing."

His face lit up. "But it does. The author and editors' houses both mysteriously burned down in the night, and people have raised memorials in the ashes where they once stood. There are too many for the guards to stop them without starting a riot."

A key clicked in a lock not too far away.

"I've got to go," he whispered. "Keep fighting."

A squad of guards entered the hall just as he rounded the far corner. They dragged me from my cell and marched me to the upper levels, until we stood in the dark hall before the gates to the arena, waiting for the previous fight to be over.

"Don't I get a weapon?" I asked.

They just laughed, until the sound was drowned out by the noise of the arena. A human scream, followed by the roar of a beast. Then dead silence, followed by the clank of iron as gates lifted so the arena could be cleaned for me.

"I've got her," said a familiar voice.

The guard who had given me the news.

He grabbed me by the shoulders and dragged me down the hall. The gates were soon before us. I tried not to notice the blood in the sand of the arena.

"Take this," he whispered, and something steel was pressed into my palms.

The handle of a dagger. I hid the knife in my boot.

"Turn around," he ordered, loud enough for others to hear.

Then he whispered: "I need to put these on you, but they won't be too tight."

He secured cuffs around my wrists.

"What am I fighting?" I asked.

"Dunno. I think-"

He snapped to attention, and shoved me to my knees, snatching the cuffs at my wrists.

The Queen was making her way down the hall, holding up the ends of her pristine dress so as not to touch the grubby floor. Like everything else in the arena, it was a relic from a past era. It looked like something a rich woman might have worn centuries ago, perhaps in the Victorian era. A bustle exaggerated the size of the Queen's ass, while a corset compressed her abdomen.

Her expression of disgust was wildly out of place with the beauty of her outfit. I must have really been annoying her if she was willing to brave the muck of the arena to speak to me.

"This is your last fight, rebel," she said, standing over me.

"You sure?" I asked. "That's what they said the first time. And the second. And the third."

I stood, and the Queen stepped back ever so slightly. But she didn't have the guards restrain me again.

"I'm certain. I've seen your opponents; I selected them myself." She smiled. "They violate the historical tradition of this arena, but every now and then we must modernize tradition to suit modern needs."

As if the security drones and robots didn't already bring modern technology to this place. But the barbaric nature of the fights here ensured everything still felt very primitive and ancient.

When I didn't look satisfactorily frightened, the Queen leaned closer to me.

"And we found your allies in the North, little rebel. I've seen the base myself."

A bluff. Meant to throw me off. We had specifically been struggling to find any sympathy in the arctic regions. It was too damn cold up there for folks to worry about much more than food and firewood.

If this was the level she was stooping to, I must have become quite a problem for her. I smiled. "That's incredible. Last I checked everyone there was pretty loyal. Figures their alliances would shift after meeting you."

She frowned, then turned to leave.

"If you survive this fight, I'll send you to the Labs, and you'll wish you were dead."

The dagger was heavy in my boot. I would rather take my own life than let her have it.

"We'll see about that."

She left, flanked by her guards, and I was walked closer to the gates. The arena was different today. There were obstacles all over the place. Wooden beams stood vertical in the ground and big boulders were scattered throughout.

There were more spectators today than ever before. They stood when the Queen entered the arena, then sat when she did. At least, most did. Some remained sitting when she entered, much to her chagrin. But it was so hard to put down little rebellions without inciting larger ones.

She settled on the velvet couch in her designated box, separated from the violence by graceful metal bars.

The guard who had given me the news stood beside me in front of the closed gate. In the time before the gate raised open, I stepped over the handcuffs so they were in front of my body. I had seen it done before, but it was harder than it looked. I fell sideways into the muck, but the guard grabbed me by the shoulder and helped me to my feet as the bars raised up.

"Thank you," I whispered as I stepped out of the shadows and into the sun.

The crowd was silent as I walked to the center of the arena. They usually cheered as the victims entered the arena in anticipation of blood, gore, and good old-fashioned entertainment. But the arena was so quiet I could hear my own ragged breathing.

I raised my hands over my head, showing the chains. People began to boo. Guards moved into place throughout the stadium, trying in vain to silence the people.

The people didn't stop. Some stood, ignoring that the Queen was seated and they were supposed to sit as well.

The armed men and women around the arena looked to the Queen. She pointed at the gate, and the nearest guard muttered orders into his radio. The guards in the stadium stepped back as the battle gates opened. She wanted me to die, so the rebellion would die with me.

My opponents charged out. Bright white fluff caught the sunlight. Were those sheep? I was supposed to be killed by sheep?

Even with my hands bound, I didn't think I had much to fear.

But as they charged closer, I saw how they ran with their heads lowered, each movement calculated and strong. These weren't just sheep. They were rams.

Ewes were meek and gentle, and raised their lambs under the care of shepherds. Rams were the ones who protected the flock when the shepherd didn't. When they leapt, they could clear any fence. When they charged, they battered down everything in their path.

Five rams ran out before the gate fell shut. Everything about them was enormous, from their curled horns down to their hooves.

Unnaturally so. They were too tall, too muscular. They tore around the pen, investigating the new space, pawing the ground.

For a moment, they just ran in circles around the large space, hooves kicking up blood-stained sand.

Then I saw they were circling around me. Froth dripped from their mouths.

I ran to the nearest boulder, and scrambled to the top. They circled the bottom, spitting and pawing at the ground.

These were not normal rams. These were hybrids. This was the sort of monstrosity that came out of the Queen's Labs. This is what she had been referring to when she said this fight would 'modernize traditions.'

It was hard to tell what they were, or used to be. Clearly they were part ram, but there was something else. There had to be.

One of them locked eyes with me, and then I knew. They were part human, or what used to be human. There was an intelligence in there, trying to best figure out how to overcome the current problem (I was out of reach) in order to complete an objective (kill me).

One of the hybrids stood at the base of a wooden platform, and let the others use himself as a step stool. One by one, the other four hybrids took a running leap, kicked up off the stepstool, and reached the nearest platform.

I pulled out my dagger, and the crowd roared, cheering for me. But I doubted one knife would save me from the Queen's monsters.

I looked around at my opponents. The fifth ram, the stepstool, remained on the ground, ensuring I couldn't escape by leaping down. I raised my knife, waited until he was in position below me, and threw it.

My aim was perfect. It buried itself in the flesh of his hindquarters, staining the wool red.

I waited for him to bleat in pain, or look back at his injury, or maybe fall over. Or at least stumble.

But he didn't even notice. He continued to walk laps around my boulder, trapping me here. And now I didn't even have a weapon.

Around and around I turned, looking for some hope

of survival. Then my eyes rose to the crowd.

Now I understood the obstacles. These were things to climb, things to hide behind. The Queen knew I couldn't survive these creatures. It was true, even with that dagger the guard had given me. The best I could hope for was to outrun them for a while.

That was what the Queen wanted. She didn't just want me to die, she wanted me pummeled to death as I cowered. She wanted me to be humiliated.

She wanted her people to watch their rising hero beaten to death by sheep.

Well, I wouldn't play that game. I held my hands above my head, showing the chains again.

I lowered myself to my knees on top of the boulder. I was going to die, and I wasn't going to do it according to plan. I wouldn't hide from her monsters.

The hybrids encircled me, jumping with unnatural grace from platform to rock until I was surrounded on every level.

The one who had stayed on the first platform was pacing, calculating the jump to my boulder. There was rage in his eyes. It was primitive, beastly. But there were other emotions in there too. Fear, regret, sadness, pain.

He lowered his head and took several steps back, preparing to charge and make the leap.

I lowered my head. I didn't want the crowds to see my fear. There was shouting. I heard the rapid hoofbeats of the hybrid, and I knew it was almost over.

I thought a hasty prayer to Fioni, wishing luck for her. I hoped she proved Bry wrong, that she show him how individuals can make a difference.

I hoped my end was quick. That some natural part of the hybrids would still understand mercy, some part that hadn't been corrupted by the Queen's Labs.

Hoofbeats scraped rock, then there was a thud. A gunshot echoed across the arena. I felt nothing. I hadn't been struck. I waited another moment, as more shouting filled the arena.

There was a desperate panting beside me. I raised my head, and saw the hybrid lying beside me. I scrambled away, then I saw the blood staining his wool. Bullet wounds.

In the arena, chaos had erupted. The young guard leaned against the railing above the arena, his gun still raised.

The other guards were moving to attack him, but a tide of civilians held them back. Some guards fired on them; others lowered their weapons. A handful set their sights on the rest of the hybrids, and on those guards who still remained loyal to their tyrant Queen.

A faint baa brought my gaze down to the hybrid on the rock. I took a step closer.

He was dying. His breaths shortened; his eyes were wild. He knew it was the end. Yet he let my hand stroke his forehead, and rested one of his massive hooves against my knee.

A part of him, some corner of his warped mind that remained pure, was grateful for the release. Grateful to no longer be another subject under the Queen's thumb.

He closed his eyes and took one last shuddering breath. I gave him a pat on the nose and stood.

I looked up at the seats of the arena, and the battle unfolding there. The Queen was nowhere to be seen. No doubt she had fled. Her soldiers were trained and armed, but there were so many more civilians here, and all of them were hell-bent on insurrection.

I stood in the center of the arena, the epicenter of chaos.

I had brought the rebellion.

Bad Vibes
Debby Feo

Something is wrong
Sensed the mother cat
Gathered her kittens
Exited Titanic

Ghost Planet
Randall Andrews

Seeing Jen alive, I'm relieved. Then confused.

When I ordered her into the escape pod, I knew I was probably sending her to her death. But the ship had seemed about to break apart. I honestly didn't expect either of us would reach the surface alive.

I scan the pod's wreckage, scattered nearby, and can't fathom how she's survived.

Then I realize Jen isn't wearing a spacesuit. Impossible!

Come to think of it, neither am I.

Even before I look behind me, I'm sure what I'll find—my ship in ruins.

> an uncharted world
> two unburied bodies
> two spirits unbound

Jamais Vu
Maureen Mancini Amaturo

The boom and thwack of the front door she knew was bolted, the scuffling of shoes that weren't hers, the crash of the frame that so carefully housed her dead husband's first love letter did not scare willful witch, Deirdre, now in her second century. "How dare you, whoever you are! Out!" she yelled, her voice rising to squeeze curdled words through a burlap throat. "Go away, I tell you. Leave me be!"

The intruder laughed. "And what will you do if I don't? You can't even see me, you old hag." Feeling invisible, the thief helped herself to Deirdre's drawer full of crystals, her pouch of coins, and her potion shelf all the while warbling a song the locals sang at solstice celebrations, full moons, and weddings. The tone suggested this housebreaker was no crone. Scabrous, shrill, and shallow this voice likely had pierced the air of no more than ninety harvest seasons.

The singing, the banging, clinking, thuds, and scrapes cued Deirdre to exactly where in the room the burglar was rifling. Without her glasses, Deirdre was feeling a bit like a corpse in a fog and reached for her wand instead of her walking stick, but as fate and force would have it, that was the right move. If she could have seen the rude fiend perfectly, she could not have made better work of it. Facing the thief's direction, she whispered, "A curse on thee to leave me be. May your spiteful gall wane weak and small."

She released a puff of magic and a bolt rendered the invader a three-legged field mouse. If she squinted, Deirdre could just about make out the slight, shadow-colored form scurrying in circles, squeaking in panic. She patted a nearby tabletop for her glasses and put them on.

"See there. You got what's coming to you." Then, her loyal cat, Jamais Vu, took over. Deirdre could tell by the smacking, scratching, chewing, and snapping that Jamais Vu was now enjoying a rich dinner.

Outside Deirdre's window, Arlynn stood in the after-dusk and mumbled, "Needles and pins! A curse on her and still I cannot get the better of this woman. What star could have granted that her magic be greater than mine?" After a covey of dawns and so many midnights, Arlynn remained a bitter and jealous sorceress, and damage done was not enough. As suns set and moons rose, she cast spells and inflictions on Deirdre, and this night's intruder was just one of many. With patient evil, still Arlynn worked to manifest her desire: that she would win the one thing Deirdre owned and magic could not tempt, the Count's true love. Yet, none of her ill intentions had come to fruition. Since using magic to murder would abolish her powers of enchantment, Arlynn decided long ago not to kill her outright and ployed other means to rid her. Should Deirdre succumb to illness or even death as a result, so mote it be. And when the moon appeared on the eve Deirdre was present no more, Arlynn would have her way. *He loved me once, so be it again*, she thought. Once more, Arlynn slipped into the night cloaked in defeat. While fading into the dark, already she tumbled plans and conjured ideas for the next curse to cast upon Dierdre — to wrong, weaken, or worse. Arlynn looked back one last time before disappearing and saw the cat watching her through the window pane. *You will be mine, my love.* She watched his back rise in a hump and his whiskers rise to bare his teeth. His eyes were fixed on her like lanterns in a dark harbor. Arlynn smiled. *Oh, yes, you will be mine.*

Inside the cottage, quiet returned. Deirdre winked at her cat and gave him a hug. "We can take care of ourselves, you and me." She nodded. "What would I have done, Jamais, if you hadn't come to me after I lost my husband?" Jamais Vu made a sorrowful sound.

With a broken heart, Deirdre maintained the day-to-day she was accustomed to while her husband was alive. She cared for their cottage. She gathered herbs. She helped heal a neighbor, set a young one on the right path, open blind eyes to true love. But the day-to-day was only that now. Without her true love, her husband, joy was scarce. Her husband was a far descendant of the Crown of Gwynedd and known as a Count, not that his status meant a hill of hyssop to her. She had fallen under the spell of his dark hair, gentle demeanor, kind heart, and romantic nature. That he treated her like the most beautiful witch in this world or the next was the bubble in the brew. They were madly in love for all of the one-hundred-plus years they were together.

Deirdre reached for her cane. Her fingertips found its gnarled surface, and she commanded it, "Come now." It rose and snuggled into her palm. She steadied herself then tapped the cane in front of her, its form awry, bent, contorted, not unlike her hands. With small steps, she doddered catawampus across the knotted wood floor until the tip of her stick tapped the broken frame that had held her husband's letter. She pushed her glasses higher on her nose and leaned closer. "There you are, my love." Relying more on magic than manual effort these days, Deirdre, her wand still in her free hand, chanted the frame into repair and back to its place on the wall. She couldn't resist reading her husband's words in that cherished love letter again, but Deirdre was distracted by her own reflection in the frame's glass. "Older, I am. And lost without my glasses these days." With her hand, she combed the cascade of chestnut waves now twined with grey. "A little baggy under the eyes." She lifted Jamais Vu and cuddled him. "He loved my eyes, he did. Said they were warm, like cognac." With her cheek pressed against the cat's, she moved her hand across the glass and traced her still firm jaw and perfectly straight nose in the reflection. "But all in all, fewer wrinkles than most my age." She placed the cat on the floor. "Don't you think, Jamais?"

Jamais Vu circled her feet. He rubbed his head up and down her leg and purred.

"At least I still have my figure...almost." She patted the folds of her well-worn frock, which did hang more loosely these days. "If the next world brings us together again, though I may be less to look at, my heart will be ready." Deirdre placed her hand on the framed letter and closed her eyes. "All I have left of you, my love." For good measure, she cast a protection spell. "Sky and sea, keep harm from thee. Earth and fire, bring my desire." She turned and waved her wand around the room. "By stars and moon and mist and moor, treasures strewn about the floor return to where I keep you stored." She heard the scraping and clanking and tinkling and listened as the wardrobe doors squeaked open and each drawer made a thud. "As it should be." Pointing to her entryway, she whispered, "Power of wind and flight of wren, doorway close secure again. Bolts and locks repair and mend." Metal clinked. Wood thumped. She reached for her cat and lifted him to her chest. "We'll be fine, me and you, Jamais Vu." The cat rubbed his ears against her lips. "We have each other."

Deirdre placed Jamais Vu on the floor and touched the framed letter again. "If only I had gone to that new moon feast with you. I should have been there, my love. I should have. But the universe set me to task with curing our cherished friend on the very same night. I remember how you so dearly wanted me to help him. Put others above yourself, you did." She shook her head. "Magic failed me that night, or something worse was at work." She looked at Jamais Vu. "Do you know the story, dear? I don't believe I ever told you about that night."

Jamais Vu stood against her skirts rubbing his head up and down. He stretched his paws scratching at the fabric.

"I left with my potions and herbs to help our ill friend that evening, and when I returned, my husband was gone. I never saw my love again, Jamais. Townsfolk searched, they did. Not a trace. At the next new moon, the Council concluded he had perished."

Rubbing against her leg, Jamais Vu rolled his head and mewed more loudly than he had ever mewed before.

Her husband's demise had scarred her heart, but the law of magic that prevented her from bringing him back from the dead infuriated her. There was, by order of the Universal Constitution of Wizardry and the Dyfarniad

Articles of Magic, no spell to bring back the dead. And all were forbidden to bring such a spell into being. She turned to Jamais Vu. "Thank the stars and orbits you came to me."

Deirdre bimbled back to her favorite chair, her worn shoes scratching the dry floor planks with each step. She plopped onto its velvet, peacock-colored cushions, leaned into its circled back, and rested her can against its thick, curved arm. After pawing the mouse bones into the hearth, Jamais Vu leaped onto her lap. She smoothed his fur from ears to tail. "Yes, we can take care of ourselves, you and me."

Jamais Vu wound around her arm.

"We are quite a pair."

Jamais Vu answered with purrs and mewing. He nuzzled his nose into the crook of her elbow and spewed a loud meow and a growl. "What is it that has you in a bother?" Deirdre asked. The cat stood and put his front paws on her shoulder and nudged her glasses with his nose. Looking her right in the eyes, he repeated the meow and growl. "No more fuss, now, love. Give us a hug." She stroked his head and snuggled him close. She closed her eyes. "I wish you could have met him. I wish I could bring him back to us." Deirdre kissed the top of Jamais' head. He mewed twice. Sleep drew near, and Dierdre melted into her velvet pillow. She slept, and Jamais Vu settled into the folds of her frock, nestled beneath the fringe of her shawl — awake, watchful, protective.

Moonlight gave way to dawn and dew. Jamais Vu climbed up to rub Deirdre's cheek with his whiskers. He nudged her chin with his nose. When Deirdre awoke, he jumped away and trotted to his food bowl. "I'll fix your breakfast," she said. Deirdre lifted herself from the pillowed chair. She reached for her cane. "Coming, my dear. Coming." After serving her cat, she warmed one brown egg for herself, nibbled dry bread with raspberry jam, and sipped hot dandelion tea. Then she brewed her daily morning potion: turmeric, ginger, and a touch of thunder god vine to relieve the ache in her aging knees and gnarled fingers; some St. John's wort, saffron, and chamomile to ease her grief. A dose a day, yet her grief remained.

Deirdre tied her deep-pocket apron on and slipped her heavier shawl around her shoulders. She removed her glasses and wiped them clean with the corner of her shawl before replacing them. "Be back soon, Jamais. Time to collect herbs to replenish my jars." Before leaving, she filled a new pouch with lavender and rosemary and placed it on the table closest to her husband's framed letter. "Every day, my love. I remember you every day. Still, I am yours."

Jamais Vu meowed three times and scratched at the floor.

"I'll be careful. I'll mind the oleander. No need for worry."

Circling her ankles and climbing over her shoes, Jamais Vu pawed at the hem of her skirt.

"I'll miss you, too. Go on, now. Rest easy, love. Get yourself cozy." Deirdre fastened the door's bolt behind her and toddled off to the woods.

Neither easy nor cozy, Jamais Vu growled and prowled and padded and paced from corner to corner. While he could do nothing about his situation, he knew the contents in the veined, amber glass bottle with the lapis stopper could. He had watched over the years as Deirdre cast her spells. He had listened. He remembered the power of each potion. That this bottle sat behind a closed cabinet door he couldn't open with his swift but clumsy paws caused him frustration he was not able to express, except for a hiss. Even if he could open the door, the amber bottle had a special place, far back in the cupboard, behind other potions. If only its contents could fall into his food, if only a few drops would spill within his reach, all would be reversed. He would be Deirdre's husband once more. Jamais Vu despised the jealous wench who had cast a spell on him that night.

* * *

The night of the new moon feast had passed and a grey day yawned. Deirdre was still away tending to their friend's health. While he slept in the vulnerability of the pre-dawn — when the mischief of the night and the promise of the day are vying to find their place — the Count fell victim to the magic of an ex-lover, Arlynn. She had never forgiven Deirdre for winning his affection, and jealousy seared her. Over time, magic proved no match for love. So, since her spells could not sway the Count's heart, Arlynn weighed the most vengeful options. Still in love with him, she dismissed killing him. She dismissed killing Deirdre, too, knowing if she did, no matter the method, surely the Count would know the truth, and that would do her no good. She would never win his love. And, of course, there were the repercussions of murder, losing her powers of enchantment completely as ruled by the Dyfarniad Articles and Constitution of Wizardry. Since killing either of them was not in the stars, Arlynn decided on a long-term punishment for them both. As the night of the new moon feast crawled toward dawn, she stood among the tree shadows outside their cottage window and cast her spell. "No longer man this man shall be. Fur fold around him, claws on his feet. His back be arched, his voice a purr 'til he loves me instead of her." If he and Deirdre wanted so badly to be together, she'd let them; however, not as man and wife. If Arlynn could not have this man, she decided he would no longer be a man, and with a wish and witchery, the Count became a cat.

When Deirdre returned after healing their friend, she was surprised to find their home empty and no note, no inkling of where her love could be. *Likely out for a morning walk*, she thought. Deirdre heard a sound and turned. A mist-grey cat sat atop her favorite chair, mewing, stretching his jaw, baring his teeth. His tail straight in agitation. "And where did you come from?" He calmed as she approached. She cradled him. "There, now." She looked into the cat's eyes. "Hungry?" Deirdre poured some milk for the cat and set a few berries on the floor. "I've never seen you around here before. I've never seen a cat like you in our part of the woods." She stroked his back as he ate. "I've never seen a cat quite as handsome as you." She stood. "I think I have just the name for you. Jamais Vu. Yes, that's who you are. Never seen."

When Jamais Vu licked the last of the milk from

the bowl, he ran to Deirdre and pawed at her skirt. She lifted him. "My husband is going to love you, Jamais Vu. Just as I do. Yes, I love you already." Deirdre looked Jamais Vu in the eyes. "You are a charmer, you are. There is something quite special about you."

Jamais licked her cheek, nuzzled his nose beneath her chin, and seemed to cry.

*   *   *

Deirdre returned from the woods, her pockets filled with leaves, flowers, berries, and stems. Minding the cobbled stones and thick hazel roots leading to her door, she did not see the nearby figure lurking in the mist, melting into the trees. Deirdre chanted as she approached her gate. "Myself and spirit no longer roam. Door be open to welcome me home."

She entered. "Here I am, Jamais." Her cat ran to her. "Easy, dear, while I empty my harvest." She limped to the cupboard and opened the doors.

Jamais Vu pushed his milk bowl closer to the cupboard then jumped up and stood atop a cupboard shelf. As Deirdre placed the lavender in its bottle, the thunder god vine in its bottle, and the St. John's Wort in its bottle, a deafening rumble of thunder shook the cottage. In seconds, a powerful wind slapped the walls and tree branches scraped the windows.

Certain this was the moment she would banish Deirdre and clear her path to seduce the Count, Arlynn imagined that she would call the Count her love before dawn. Outside, Arlynn stepped from behind an elm. "Elements all, I call you now. Force this wench to tremors bow. I call the earth beneath today to quake and send her far away!"

A flurry of leaves began to swirl. A tempest howled and moaned. Quavery trees buckled and bent as if unsure of their footing. A quake roiled, and the tremors caused Deirdre's floors to shift and walls to quiver. "Oh my stars, Jamais! Blessed be, I returned home just in time."

Vibrations rattled and toppled the bottles on each shelf. Jamais Vu looked up. With so many potion jars out of place waiting to be refilled, nothing stood in the way of the amber bottle. Thanks to the storm's agitation and earth's wobbling, the bottle most important to him was teetering on the shelf's edge. Thunder boomed. Deirdre startled. The amber glass bottle hit the floor, and its lapis top loosened. The liquid inside drained onto the wood. Jamais Vu leaped down and licked at the drops.

With the sky darkening and the wind battering and the lightening sparking, Deirdre scooped Jamais Vu from the floor and bundled a blanket in her arms. "Let's set ourselves safe, my love." She locked the shutters and drew the curtains. She lifted Jamais Vu, reached for her wand, and climbed into bed, pulling the blanket about them both. "Chores can wait. The earth is telling us to huddle and rest." She pet the cat's head. "Nature is amiss, my love." Deirdre waved her wand across their blanket, over their heads, and down the other side. "Elements all, I bid you hush. Make serene all nature's fuss. By stars and moon protect us well from harm within this tempest's swell. No ill, I cast, come to our souls. May light and good and peace unfold."

The rumbling weakened. The tremors slowed. The wind lost its voice. Quiet crept over the cottage, except for the tapping of the rain, gentle now. Outside, beneath the arms of the trees, Arlynn fell to her knees, her fists buried in the draping sleeves of her robe. "Again! Needles and pins! Not this day, but one day." She rose and skulked away.

In the quiet of their cottage, Deirdre cuddled Jamais Vu. "There now." She smooth her hand across his fur. "A good nap and things will be better in a little while, my love. Things will be so much better."

Jamais Vu wriggled. He preened and purred and smiled a cat's smile for the last time.

Confronting the Demon
Sandy DeLuca

Fearfully And Wonderfully

Made
Veronica Leigh

Poland

Raisel ground the heel of her right palm into the dough, working and kneading it. Sweat beaded along her brow and as it trickled down her cheek, she rubbed her face against her shoulder. A murmur of commotion outside resounded, but she disregarded it, eager to finish her chore that way she could go on her daily walk. *I just need a moment's peace.* The uncharacteristically seasonal weather beckoned, a cool wind rolled off the Vistula and through the cottage's open window, cooling her suffocating body.

The chatter intensified and the flustered tones of the folk in the village beckoned her to the window. Raisel peered out, her forehead furrowed as she watched her neighbors frantically dash into their homes and slam the doors.

The front door of the cottage swung open and her *foter* and neighbor Gavriel barreled inside. Gavriel closed the door behind him.

Raisel dusted her hands off on her apron and observing the gentlemen's troubled countenances, her heart fluttered anxiously. "What is it?" She asked.

"A Christian boy from the nearby village is missing." *Foter* pulled the shutters closed and sighed wearily, fully looking his fifth decade. He ran his fingers through his graying beard, twisting the ends of it. "Christians are swarming the countryside in search of him."

"They may find him." Raisel suggested, shedding her apron and draping it over a chair.

"They should be invading our village soon." Gavriel argued, shaking his head.

Raisel lowered her head, and knew what Gavriel meant by *they*. Whether the boy was found alive or not, the Christians would be coming for her and her people. For centuries, whenever a Christian child went missing or was killed, their little village was blamed for the crime. Never mind that her people – the Jews – had nothing to do with the matter, they were always to blame. The Christians believed that every year during Passover, the Jews would abduct a Christian child and sacrifice it to the devil, then use its blood to make *matzah*. In retaliation, mobs of Christians would come down and unleash a *pogrom* upon the village. Men, women, and children would be murdered...all because they were Jews.

The pressure of unshed tears mounted behind Raisel's eyes. *My mamah was killed in a pogrom, years ago.* Her *foter* was in Krakow for business, leaving *Mamah* and her alone when that pogrom began. She had been seven, but Raisel distinctly remembered *Mamah* leading her to the woods and coaxing her to lie down in a hollowed-out log. *Mamah* distracted the men who had come to slay, and led them off into a wild chase that ended in her demise. When it was safe, Raisel crawled out of the log and another neighbor hiding in the woods discovered her, and brought her back to the village. As the village's sole rabbi, when *Foter* returned, he had to conduct the funerals of all who perished – including his wife.

"We must gather what we can and flee to the woods." *Foter* declared.

Raisel found herself nodding, and numbly gathered up things they would need and a few sentimental belongings. She stored everything in a worn, old sack. Their clothing, food, her *foter's* books. *How many times have I done this?* Frightening as it was, she had to pack and flee numerous pogroms throughout her eighteen years. She and *Foter* had been lucky, escaping each time before the Christians came. A few days in the woods, they would return to their cottage and begin yet again.

"I shall fetch my things and be back soon." Gavriel announced and lifting his strong chin in her direction, he swept out of the cottage.

Raisel rolled her eyes. Gavriel had become close to her *foter*, offering assistance when required. She wasn't blind though or naïve; he was singling her out for marriage. But that was of little matter now.

She claimed the *Sefer Yetzirah* that had belonged to

Mamah from the shelf and was about to place it in the sack, when she paused. Running her thumb over its worn cover, she considered what she had read the night before. Customarily, boys and men were the only ones who could read. Yet *Mamah* had known how and she taught her. How her *mamah* came by this mysterious book, Raisel didn't know, but she was glad it had been shared with her. The *Sefer Yetzirah* was the only thing she had left of *Mamah*. Last night before she blew out her candle, she read the legend of the golem.

A *golem!* Raisel brushed her fingertips against her lips and placed them on the book. A golem could save them! A creature molded from clay and brought to life; it served the one who brought him into being. A golem would ensure the Christians would never harm her people again.

And as a rabbi, her *foter* should be acquainted enough with the *Kabbalah* to summon it. Only a rabbi could wield the white magic of the Jewish sages.

Raisel carried the book over to her *foter*, who was packing, and tugged on his sleeve. "*Foter*, I have been reading and studying. Since the Vistula River runs through the woods, perhaps we should try to create a golem to protect our people." When he swung around, flustered by her interruption, she chewed on her lower lip. "You are a rabbi."

Foter shot her a withering look. "My girl, don't be foolish. Now is not the time to rely on childish stories." He waved her off, as though he were waving off a dog.

"They're not childish." Raisel hugged the book to her chest.

"Golems are not real." *Foter* reiterated, his cheeks puffing out impatiently. "They are only folktales to inspire us to have courage in times of trouble. G-d expects us to rely on him for deliverance." He gestured towards her abandoned sack on the floor and ordered, "Now, pack!"

Raise recoiled and reminded herself he was upset that their lives were in danger, but his sharpness stung. Time and time again they retreated to the woods, praying to the L-rd for protection. Time and time again her people were slaughtered while G-d looked the other way. *At least that's how it feels.* Perhaps the golem was only a folk story, but at this point, what did they have to lose by attempting to create one?

While *Foter's* back was to her, Raisel slipped the *Sefer Yetzirah* into her sack, vowing to attempt to persuade him again when they reached the woods.

* * *

Raisel trembled as she trudged through the softened earth bordering the Vistula River, feeling her feet sink lower with each step she took. *Foter* and Gavriel ordered her to remain hidden in a cave while they tried to help others escape the pogrom. But she believed if the Christians were hunting Jews down, a cave would be the first place they would look. *Besides, I cannot sit idly by while my people suffer.* A hint of smoke tickled her nostrils and her eyes watered, knowing the Christians were burning her village. Their blood cried out louder than their screams. The sack containing *Sefer Yetzirah* slung over her shoulder bounced against her spine with every movement. *I have to do something! I shall have to make the golem myself.* The sun had begun its descent and night would soon fall, leaving her and the others far more vulnerable. She had to hurry before it was too late.

The cluster of trees surrounding her offered a wall of protection, but obstructed what daylight she had left. Building a fire was out of the question, that would only draw attention and spoil her plan.

This is it. Raisel decided and knelt on the embankment of the river. Laying the sack aside, she dug her fingers through the pliable clay soil and diligently worked at forming the shape of a man. *No different than kneading bread.* There wasn't enough time to build a large golem, he wasn't much bigger than she was, but stature was unimportant. According to folklore, he would wield powers and possess magical abilities. It was written that the golem could become invisible, he would attack, and he was able to call upon the spirits of the dead to annihilate.

Sitting back on her heels, she observed the mold and was satisfied with her work. It was the best she could do under such circumstances. Using her fingernail, she scratched the word *emet* on the golem's brow. It meant truth.

Raisel wiped her filthy hands on her skirt and when she was clean enough, she scrounged through the sack, pulling out the book, and a set of clothes and boots that belonged to her *foter*. Leaving the clothing on top of the sack, she rose, holding the *Sefer Yetzirah* and opened it to the chapter she needed. *Please, let this work.* Raisel pleaded, unsure if she was speaking to herself or the L-rd. Circling her creation seven times, she reverently uttered the Name of G-d. She had discovered the Name in one of her numerous readings of the golem tale and committed it to memory, not daring to invoke *It* until now.

After completing her seventh circle, Raisel froze in place, sensing an abrupt change in her surroundings. The moon chased off the sun and its light, ushering in a black sky. Its white-gold beams were the only source of illumination. But it was enough. Birds were silenced, the squirrels scattered, the Vistula's current appeared to cease. The gentle breeze transformed into a gale and her head began to pound as it did when gusts drifted off the Tatra Mountains.

Raisel's mind harkened back to the story *Mamah* used to tell her of Elijah the Prophet, one she committed to memory. *"the* LORD *passed by, and a great and strong wind rent the mountains, and brake in pieces the rocks before the* LORD; *but the* LORD *was not in the wind: and after the wind an earthquake; but the* LORD *was not in the earthquake: And after the earthquake a fire; but the* LORD *was not in the fire: and after the fire a still small voice."*

"Awake!" Raisel shouted at the clay form.

Her eyes widened at the sight of the clay transforming into man. *It is working!* He sat up and then pushed himself to his feet. Whilst his skin was reddish and reddened with each passing second, he resembled a normal man in many ways. Eyes, ears, nose, mouth, and a crop of unruly hair. His body was that of a man's too, he was bare and he knew no shame.

The golem moved his head, his eyes narrowing, as he studied the area...His expression was a cross between befuddlement and awe. He tilted his head, his gaze settling on her.

"I am Raisel, daughter of Rabbi Michael and I have created you." Raisel announced, and she then blushed, unable to ignore the obvious. She grabbed the set of clothing she had waiting, thrusting it at him to cover himself. Then she handed off the boots. "Here, wear these." She ordered.

If the moon had been brighter, she would have known for certain. But she could swear she noticed a glimmer of a smirk on the golem's face. The golem obeyed her and dressed, then shoved his feet into the boots. Once more, he gave her his undivided attention.

"My people are in danger." Raisel declared and prayed he would understand the dire situation she and her village were in. "I ask you to protect the ones you hear screaming. Please, don't let any more of them perish. Go, and when you are finished, return to me."

At first the golem didn't move, eyeing her. Then he slowly nodded, and he moved in the direction of her village.

Raisel watched his retreating form, wishing she could follow. But she had to find *Foter* and Gavriel and tell them all that occurred. She couldn't wait to reveal her creation to them.

* * *

Neither *Foter* or Gavriel believed Raisel when she shared what had transpired. Even when she showed them the man-shaped indentation in the ground from the golem had lain. *Foter* was upset that she disobeyed him, Gavriel believed she had fallen asleep and dreamt of the golem. Both men scolded her endlessly for venturing out of the cave and endangering herself.

Raisel pressed her lips together, enduring the admonitions, believing it was useless to try and reason with them. *They will believe me, once they see him.* The cries of her people began to die down, and peace swept through the village and extended into the woods. For her it was reassurance that the golem had intervened and the pogrom was ending.

A proud smile broke out on her face when she

detected the golem's familiar stride as he moved through the woods and approached her. The golem stopped before Raisel, and she nodded to him approvingly. His clothing was splattered with blood and her gaze traveled the length of him, detecting blood staining his fingers and boots. But, she reasoned, his actions were justified as he was protecting the innocent.

Foter's stern words died on his tongue when he clamped eyes on the golem. His jaw slackened, and he visibly blanched.

Gavriel staggered backwards, colliding into a birch tree. He then scrambled around it and hid behind its trunk.

"What is that?" *Foter's* arm quivered as he raised it and pointed it at her creation.

"A golem." Raisel was beaming, holding her head high. She crossed her arms and rocked back and forth proudly on her heels. "I made him."

"Y-you?" Gavriel sputtered, from his hiding place.

Raisel nodded. "Yes." She closed the gap between her and the golem, realizing that he needed a proper name. Creating him had made her feel godlike...or rather goddess-like. There was only one name suitable for him. "Thank you...Adam." Despite his crimson-stained hands, she claimed one of his hands and squeezed it gratefully.

Adam didn't respond and then she remembered as in the folktale, he likely couldn't speak. Yet there was softness in his eyes and his smile. As G-d knew man's thoughts, Raisel believed she mystically could understand Adam's thoughts and feel his emotions. The tumultuous weather from earlier had calmed, the delicate balance of nature restored now that creator and creature stood united.

Foter soon joined Gavriel behind the birch tree and though she couldn't make out their hushed exchange, she could hear it was heated.

"Come, Adam, let us go home." Raisel led the golem by the hand to the village, eager to parade her miraculous creation before her people.

* * *

Whilst the majority of the village had been spared from the pogrom, and her neighbors would be able to salvage their livelihoods, Raisel couldn't shake off the feeling that she was being shunned.

I am not imagining it. Raise frowned, as she and Adam passed by the baker. She nodded to the man, greeting him politely. The baker averted his gaze and scurried back into what remained of his business. She glanced at Adam, who offered her an encouraging smile in return. *Never mind, it doesn't matter.* Though she was willing to fetch her own water from the well, Adam – in his own quiet manner – persisted in toting the heavy pail for her.

But it did matter. Their rejection stung. She had done the impossible and created a golem, for her neighbors' sakes. And Adam defeated those that sought to harm her people. The locals could at least be appreciative, but instead they were wary of Adam...and of her. Their lives were saved, but she had done what was forbidden. The mysticism she uncovered and used in Adam's creation, was forbidden to her sex. Girls and women were required to follow tradition, and she ventured out of that small world constructed for her.

On reaching the threshold of her cottage, Raisel kissed her fingertips and then touched the mezuzah affixed to the doorpost. Adam switched the pail, from his right to his left, and mimicked her gesture.

Raisel stopped short though when she found *Foter* and Gavriel flanking the table, as though they were awaiting her return. Her eyes dropped to the cup of wine. *The betrothal cup.* She sighed, her shoulders sagging. Gavriel called often and he and *Foter* continually had private talks, excluding her. It was her life and her fate, yet she was not consulted.

Adam dropped the pail on the floor. The momentum made the water slosh over the rim, but no one was paying close attention to that. He positioned himself at her side, his arms folded, staring down Gavriel.

"The beast is still here?" Gavriel narrowed his cool blue eyes, leaving her chilled inside.

"He is not a beast and his name is Adam." Raisel

countered. She could grudgingly accept that those in the village opposed Adam. They didn't understand, they were frightened of the unknown. But she would have thought Gavriel, who was devoted to her and her *foter*, would be more accepting. "Where else should he be?"

Gavriel's jaw clenched tightly. He was not accustomed to her – a woman - questioning his authority. "Now that the Christians are no longer a threat, I assumed we would no longer have any use for him."

"You have assumed wrong." Raisel replied.

Foter, who had been peculiarly quiet until this point, finally spoke up. "Gavriel has come to ask for your hand in marriage." The apples of his cheeks reddened over his graying beard, indicating that he too wasn't used to her speaking out of turn. However, there was a first time for everything. "And I have granted his request."

Raisel scrutinized Gavriel. A handsome young man, he was ruddy and tall, his character was good. Many of the girls in the village eyed him, eager for him to turn his attention towards them. Yet he chose her, a girl far more comfortable buried in a book, studying the *Kabbalah* and forming creatures out of clay. Despite Gavriel's wishes, and her *Foter's*, and the customs of her people, she wouldn't make a proper wife. Keeping house and raising a family, none of that appealed to her. For the first time in her life, she felt alive. G-d would understand; He had enabled her to wield this power, He created her like this as she had created Adam.

I will not forfeit my freedom, nor will I forfeit Adam. For she knew, if she agreed to Gavriel and *Foter's* plan, Adam would be rendered back to clay. And they would be able to control her once more. She cast a glance at the golem, and meeting his gaze, she was emboldened by his presence. Others might not support her, but he would.

Raisel shook her head. "Neither of you asked me, and unless I drink from the cup, there will be no betrothal or marriage." Dismissing their ploy with a wave of her hand, she stated: "I refuse to partake."

Foter blinked in astonishment. She couldn't fault him for doing what any good Jewish *foter* would do for his daughter: arrange a marriage to ensure she was cared for. Generations had done so before him, generations would after him. Her *foter* was old. A head full of graying hair, his face was round, as was his body. His movements had slowed over the last year, and it had become a challenge to lead the village spiritually. No doubt he wanted her in a secure marriage before he departed from this world and was accepted in *Olam Ha-ba*. Even so, she could not live a life unsuitable for her.

"Gavriel is a good, honorable, and respectable man." *Foter* insisted. He approached, and cupped her shoulder, squeezing it gently. It was the closest he ever came to showing affection. Her *mamah* was the one who bestowed all of the hugs and kisses in her childhood. "He would provide well for you. You are in your eighteenth year and in desperate need of a husband."

"No, I am not." Raisel locked eyes with her *foter*, praying he would at last comprehend.

Gavriel sharply advanced towards her. Whether he intended to whisper something privately to her, or touch her, he never got the chance.

Adam sleekly moved like a cat, and bringing his hand up to Gavriel's broad chest, the force knocked the latter backwards. Gavriel was slammed against the wall behind, crushing wood. The cottage trembled from the momentum.

Raisel gasped, not from horror, but from amazement. Adam barely laid a finger on Gavriel, but the strength he harnessed in a simple movement was miraculous. Yet his eyes were dilated to the point of looking feral, and his nostrils flared.

Gavriel shook off the attack, and crawling a few paces, he unsteadily rose to his feet. His muscular body left behind an impression on the wooden wall. Before another word could be uttered, or before Adam could defend her again, Gavriel scrambled past them and out of the cottage.

"Raisel!" *Foter* retreated from her, as though she had been the one to assault Gavriel. Perhaps, in a sense he was right. More or less, through her creation and bidding, Adam acted on her behalf. "How could you shame me like that?" He tisked his tongue. "This golem-" *Foter* hissed the word as though it were profane, "this power you have wielded has corrupted you. You must destroy him before he destroys you."

"Never." Raisel said.

According to her studies, only the one who created the golem could end him. Despite *Foter*, Gavriel, and the villages' desire to destroy Adam, they couldn't. They didn't know how. Even if they did, they were too frightened to be near him.

Though it was strictly forbidden for women and men to touch, Raisel linked her arm through Adam's, and led him out of the cottage.

* * *

Raisel didn't stop until she and Adam came to the Vistula River, the location he was created in. The recent rains flatted down the area where she molded the clay and he rose from the earth. Still, she would never forget the place where this all began. *There is something holy about this part of the woods.* She crouched down on the embankment and unlacing her boots, she stripped the stockings off of her feet and dangled her feet in the cool waters. Peering up at Adam, she patted the spot on her right, and was pleased when he sat with her.

Despite the insults *Foter* and Gavriel made against him, Adam was unfazed by what had occurred at the cottage. Most of the legends insisted golems were simple creatures without a thought of their own. But in regards to Adam, Raisel was convinced it was untrue. He was mute, but he had a mark of intelligence, he displayed emotions and loyalty. In time, she believed he would continue to develop and become independent of her. He would live as any other man.

"I am sorry, Adam, for how they have treated you." Raisel sighed and grasped his hand, compressing it gently. "My *foter* isn't a bad man; he wants what every *foter* wants for his daughter. But after creating you, I know I won't be satisfied with an ordinary life. I wish we could run away and travel the world together." She hazarded a glance at him, and didn't detect any condemnation.

Adam nodded patiently. The longer she gazed upon him, she marveled at how fearfully and wonderfully made he was. His eyes were like orbs of amber one could collect on shores and fashion into jewelry. His skin was reddish, darker and deeper than the clay he had been made from, and his complexion was mottled, but whenever she touched him, his skin was the texture of hers. Adam's unruly crop of hair looked soft and inviting, and she yearned to comb her fingers through it.

There is no difference between us. Raisel reasoned. In a sense, she and her people were also golems. G-d created the original man from the dust of the earth and breathed life into him. Like the L-rd, she created Adam in her own image. He had a free will of his own. She and Adam were equals in every sense of the word.

Inclining her head, she brushed her lips against his. The kiss lasted only a second, and when she drew back, she was mortified. "I'm sorry," Raisel regretfully squeezed her eyes closed. "I never asked you what you wanted, or what you feel, or what you are thinking. I-"

Her lashes fluttered when she felt his palm on her upturned cheek and her breathing grew shallow as Adam brushed his mouth against hers. Blood thrummed through her veins; her limbs tingled. It was their own brand of mysticism not foretold in the book.

Gavriel never made me feel like this.

Raisel rested her brow against Adam's. They would briefly return to the cottage, for her to gather her belongings. Then she and Adam would leave the village and spend the rest of their days exploring the world.

* * *

Dark, low hanging clouds gathered above and the wind picked up as Raisel and Adam reentered the village, hand in hand. If the abrupt turn in the weather was any indication, she ought to have sensed what lay ahead of them. But it wasn't until her neighbors stirred from their cottages and trailed after her and Adam as they headed home. Her grip on Adam tightened, relying on him for strength. *They oppose us...they oppose Adam.* She concluded, keeping her head low, to avoid challenging anyone.

Raisel halted, as did Adam, when she found Gavriel waiting for her by the cottage. *Foter* was off to the side, anxiously wringing his hands.

"What is this?" Raisel lifted her hand, palm upwards, gesturing to those who surrounded them.

"We have talked and we agree this golem is a danger to our village." Gavriel glared in Adam's direction, the corner of his mouth up turning into a satisfied smirk.

With the exception of defending her from Gavriel's advances, Adam never once resulted in unsanctioned violence. Even with his freedom of thought and free will, he acted accordingly to her wishes. He served the village faithfully, though the neighbors refused to fully accept him. The mob that had congregated, had swiftly turned against Adam, forgetting the past.

"How can you say that?" Raisel surveyed the crowd and whilst she would attempt to reason with them, she knew it was futile. They believed what they wanted to believe. "Adam saved you from the pogrom. How could you betray him?"

Adam outwardly flinched. He understood precisely what was happening. However, he offered no resistance to the villagers. To offer him a bit of comfort, she clung to his arm.

Foter protested, "He attacked Gavriel, he is a menace, and he is out of control." He cautiously broached her, as if hesitant of Adam and his might. "And your actions in creating him were unholy. Only a rabbi can harness such power." He lowered his tone, speaking loud enough for only her to hear. "Some fear you are a witch." *Foter* let out a moan. "Please, daughter, I cannot have you killed for being a witch!"

Raisel's mouth dropped. As the rabbi of the village, he ought to have been the one to explore the *Kabbalah* and create the golem. He would have been justified, the village would have supported him, and he would have been hailed as a savior. But because she was a woman and she had dared to step out of her place in society, she was cursed as a witch. And now that she would not submit to her *foter* and thwarted suitor, she was being condemned. Those unfamiliar with the unknown and the unusual were terrified of it. Neither she nor Adam would be accepted there. They were right in running away.

"But you know me." Raisel argued. "You have known me my whole life. No, please, Adam is my only friend."

Her logic fell on deaf ears. The villagers may have known her since she was a girl, but they stared her down as though she truly did dabble in the dark arts.

"You love this golem?" Gavriel scoffed, then gritting his teeth, he snarled, "We have decided that you destroy him, or we will."

Raisel was about to warn them that they could not destroy Adam. They didn't know how. If Gavriel or anyone attacked him, or tried to subdue her, Adam would annihilate the entire village. Whatever pogrom the Christians intended would be small compared to what Adam would unleash. If she and Adam attempted to leave, they would pursue her. Adam would retaliate and her *foter* and her former friends would die. And she couldn't allow that.

Raisel stepped before Adam and studied his countenance one last time, memorizing every feature, she noted his sad, but tranquil expression. His amber eyes were glassy, as though they were about to shed tears. Despite his own feelings, he nodded his head, giving her permission to what was necessary.

Raising her hand, she thumbed one of the letters from Adam's brow, smoothing it out. No longer did it say *emet*, it said *met*. That meant death.

Raisel wept as she watched the golem sink to the ground and lay back, the breath of life leaving his body. His eyes closed. *He is dead.* Made of clay, his form began to crumble and turn back to dust. A stray wind of the *halny* swept through the village, and carried the particles away. Only the clothing Adam wore remained.

Foter's heavy footfalls neared and he placed his hand on her shoulder. "I know you are upset, but someday you will understand-"

Raisel flinched, and shirked from his touch. She stalked past her *foter,* Gavriel, and her neighbors and entered the cottage, slamming the door behind her. Fetching the sack she had used during the pogrom, she placed the *Sefer Yetzirah* inside, along with her other belongings. *Foter* and Gavriel may have destroyed one bit of happiness, but she wouldn't allow them to decide her fate. She would keep her promise to Adam, to run away and travel the world.

But before she left entirely, she would return to the Vistula River, where she created Adam...and she would create him again. Then everything would be as it should be.

* * *

Raisel closed the *Sefer Yetzirah* and laid the book down on the sack on the ground. *Why isn't it working?* She sank next to the newly formed golem she had molded into being. *I have done everything the same!* Lifting her eyes to the pitch-black sky, she looked to the yellow-gold moon peering between the tree tops. She left after *Foter* turned in for the night, creeping out of their cottage, vowing to never return. Escaping from the village, she headed directly to the area by the Vistula River, where Adam was created. She molded a similarly shaped form, wrote the word *truth* on his brow, circled him seven times intoning the Name of G-d, praying as fervently as her spirit would allow. Yet the white magic of the Jewish sages, the *Kaballah*, failed. *I failed.*

She used her sleeve to wipe the tears from her cheeks. To recreate Adam was impossible. There was only one Adam, just as the L-rd created only one of her. The creation of the golem the first time, it was a spiritual experience. Adam came into being when her people needed him most...when she needed him most. His presence emboldened her, he made her realize she would never be satisfied following tradition. *I am meant for something else.* And now she was free.

Raisel sniffed, wiped her face once more, and then rose. She put the *Sefer Yetzirah* back in the sack, and slung the sack over her shoulder. Adam's spirit was out there, somewhere. Or rather, it was within her since she was the creator of him. Perhaps in her travels, she would once more feel close to him.

Spaced Out
Debby Feo

Bird got out
Cat got out
Bird flew to shoulder
Cat leaped to shoulder

Owner down
Holes in suit
Air leaked out punctures
Woman's face turned blue

A Nice Girl Like You
Tyree Campbell

"She just sat down at the corner table," said Big Gooey.

I braced myself with a slug of bootleg Jameson's before turning my head discreetly toward Tsebieh. "She looks human," I said, after he had wiped the counter around my drink with a flourish. The maneuver failed to repair the maculate condition of the faux hardwood.

"DNA splice," explained Big Gooey, as he probed his ear with the point of a tusk the size of my forearm. He looked strong enough to have removed it from the creature while it was still alive. His mustache bristled, the last twitch of a sepia burrowing animal that had crawled onto Gooey's lip only to succumb to his breath. "Experimental thing. She shoulda died."

I looked again. Tsebieh was not of that physical type which invites second glances. She was sitting on a bench at a window booth on this side of the Universe, at just enough angle for me to catch the tiny downward curls of the corners of her mouth while a stevedore from a galleon newly arrived at the Spaceport braced an arm on the table and broached his offer. Nobody ever fell in love here in the *Tarry A'Dea*, but now and then some of the patrons tumbled into lust. Anyone could see from the expression on her face that she was having none of it--anyone except the stevedore. As he leaned down, placing more weight on his arm, Tsebieh made a little move quicker than my eye could follow, and in the next instant the stevedore's chin cracked on the tabletop and the wrist of that arm was in her grasp just above the debris-cluttered floor. She had slender, pale fingers, delicate-looking in the shadows under the table, yet clearly she held his limb in a grip of iron. Her mouth moved, and words whistled just far enough to reach his ears and his alone. Then she released him, and he departed, rather more swiftly than he had arrived, blood welling through the gash in his chin and dripping onto his traveled gray pullover, where it added to an unsavory retinue of other stains.

"Does she ever say 'yes' to anyone?" I asked Big Gooey.

For an instant Gooey's eyes darkened to tangerine, and I knew I'd asked a borderline question. Everyone has a history. Those who don't want theirs probed sometimes migrate out here to Chthonia, living *ad hoc* lives, unable for a variety of reasons to return to their worlds of origin, and he was wondering whether I'd meant to violate the no-pry rule. Then the eyes reverted to their normal color, not quite lemon, not quite pus, and under the mustache his thick lips parted in what was, for him, a flicker of amusement.

"Depends on the question, Mac."

I'd seen no need to burden him with Emer Bridget McClafferty, which is what appeared on the natal documents long ago and far away, or with any of the other names I'd adopted during the subsequent thirty-seven Standard years. Big Gooey would presume an alias no matter what I gave him, and "Mac" was generic enough to render plausible, if necessary, a case of mistaken identity.

Nursing the first two drinks, I hadn't revealed what it was I wanted to ask Tsebieh, only that I had need of assistance from someone of her reputed talents. It was unnecessary to add a wink and a nudge. Big Gooey knew damn well what I was referring to, and he wanted in the worst way to ask me just how the hell I'd come to know about her, but he, too, had to maintain the no-pry protocols, although, being a bartender, he was permitted considerable leeway.

I scanned the rack of tins against the wall behind him. "Warm up a bowl of *gretel*, please. And side it with some of those crackers."

Big Gooey's eyebrows merged like rutting caterpillars as he fulfilled the request, setting the nuke to a proper 356 degrees Kelvin and the timer to twenty five seconds. I spread three small silver coins on the countertop, and as the nuke signaled the end of its programmed task they disappeared into Gooey's huge paw. Whatever his opinion of my imminent ploy, he would not interfere.

The uncovered stoneware tureen Gooey presented me on a saucer contained a viscous brick-red liquid full of pink and reseda vermiform chunks. Proper *gretel* resembles nothing so much as "entrail stew," and although this had come from a tin, it retained the pungent, distinctive odor of decomposition. Gingerly I carried the tureen and its steaming repast to her table, and noted the do-not-disturb frown with which she greeted me.

She had the rich voice of a cello, played with a taut steel bow. "I ordered nothing."

"This is for me."

She arched one auburn eyebrow at me, her only response.

I remained standing. "I can't remember whether you mix the crackers into the *gretel*, or eat them separately. I was hoping you'd know."

She gave me a five-count. "It makes no difference."

"Thanks. I didn't want to insult the meal by---"

"Sit down."

I did so. After another pause, Tsebieh said, "*Gretel* probably won't do you any harm, but I doubt you'll like it."

"So you think I should just eat the crackers?"

"You've done your homework."

"Some of it. Not enough. Would you care for this, then?"

She gazed out into the moonless night, her pale eyes shadowed by the infinite black and by a past I could only guess at. You don't escape from GenTail's Abyss without killing someone. Even someone with her gifts would have to dispatch the field generator tech.

"It's not magic, what I do," Tsebieh said, still fixed on the blackness. Her words spilled onto my ears like spring rain, just before the flowers come up. If I hadn't remembered she possessed an alimentary canal capable of digesting *gretel*, I might have been entranced. "It's mathematical. That's why the field generator works. There are limitations. I can only go to places I've been, or seen, or have a clear vision of. And I must be in physical contact with the world of their location. And no, I don't read minds. They had developed the DNA splice for that, but upon further consideration realized that their own minds would become transparent as well. Possibly one day they'll develop a splice that will enable someone to block a mind probe..." Suddenly her eyes widened. Then, turning back to me, she said very softly, "No. Besides, all the data for the telepathy splice is on computer. No hard copies. And the computer is absolutely impenetrable. It's the ultimate no-hacking zone. There's even a dampening field surrounding it, a countermeasure against explosives."

Tsebieh was talking too much. I wondered how long she had examined the possibilities from all angles, weighing this method of entry against that, measuring obstacles against her abilities, until futility set in. She'd begun life as a vegetable, and now, on Chthonia, she was regressing to that mental state.

Slowly, almost imperceptibly, the tureen of *gretel* slid across the tabletop to her...and vanished, as did she. But she left me the crackers.

*   *   *

Like taverns everywhere that cater to clandestine activities limited by various ill-conceived statutes, the *Tarry A'Dea* let rooms on its second level for various periods of time, some measured in minutes, some in years. During prolonged absences from their normal surroundings, people become lonely or bored, and biological relief without the complications of emotional attachments can be had, like any other goods or services, for a price. [You pay someone to cut your hair, right? Although you could cut it yourself, someone else, properly trained, makes a better job of it, right?] On the way to the stairs and up, I received no less than three come-hithers, including one from a young woman whose maculate attire and disheveled condition clearly bespoke a desperation for funds. Passing her by, I scrawled a mental note to have Big Gooey present her with a complimentary meal or two, and arrange for her to "find" a couple leafs of folded currency. As to the other offers, while I certainly appreciate a man who comes and goes, I was not in the mood. Tsebieh had vanished from the booth, but now that we had established contact, however tenuous, she might pop in at any time. And there are some activities that should not be popped-in upon.

I'd taken a room at the far end of the hallway, next to the emergency exit--events that constitute emergencies are not limited to fires, and in my line of work it's always prudent to have multiple escape routes. The touchpad on the wall beside the doorjamb accepted the code Gooey had given me, and as the door slid open the traditional odors of old exhalations, stale love, and something edible left out too long whistled past me and down the hallway like liberated ghosts. A dim ceiling panel began to glow at a touch to the wall pad, yielding just enough light for me to see that the single room was unoccupied and that the bed was empty, covered, and too small for two--although, to be fair, couples in this room seldom slept far apart, if at all. The single window was closed, the heavy drapes pulled, and I doubted there was enough light to silhouette me to the casual viewer outside. In the shadows of a far corner stood a rack on which I might hang my clothing, and beside that a commode and a sink. If I wanted a shower, I'd have to use the common room.

The bed squeaked when I sat down, further dampening any nocturnal ambitions I might have had. There were places in the Universe where the rhythms of life were accompanied by cheers and applause, but not here, where yielding bedsprings announced the vulnerability of one or both of the participants to anyone who would do harm. Perforce celibate, I could only wait for developments, and doze cautiously in the meantime.

I reckoned more than half the night had passed by the time Tsebieh entered. She did not use the door. In one moment I was alone, in the next she was standing before me, and in the next I had the ancient military automatic pistol out and aimed at her gut.

She withdrew a pace. "What is *that*?"

I carry a pistol because most security detectors are keyed to plastic and energy cells, not to metal, and because firing it makes enough noise to startle an adversary, a useful advantage in the event the first bullet fails to find its mark. I did not tell her this.

"Next time, knock."

Long ago Tsebieh had been developed as an alien sentient species--they'd done good work on her. The light that shone from above and behind her cast her face in delicate grays and glows, the humanizing effect startling, and I averted my eyes, blinking away the entrancement.

"I'm not going back there."

"You don't have to," I said. "Just get me inside."

"You're insane."

And I thought, *Insane is what they did to you.*

Between the booth and now she'd changed to a rugged travel outfit of cammie jacket and denims, and sturdy black boots. Chthonia is not known for ease of terrain. She'd made up her mind to flee into the hinterlands.

So why come to see me?

I patted the bed beside me. "Sit down, Tsebieh."

Given what usually took place in this room, her hesitation was understandable. But she obeyed, maintaining a discreet forearm-length of distance between us, pale eyes wary in the dim light. A hint of lilac mixed with the musk she emitted, the blend as effective as pheromones. In my research I had not considered how the spliced DNA might affect her sexuality, except to hypothesize that they would not want her to reproduce unless it was under their auspices. Now, in proximity, she became a liability to my personal and mission security.

"The firewall is impenetrable," Tsebieh said in a low voice, hands clasped between her knees as if to avoid gestures and, perhaps, physical contact. "Passwords comprise the respective DNA of those few who are authorized access. And GenTail will backtrace any attempt to access data, even to Chthonia." She turned her face toward me. Eyes the color of fresh rainwater sought answers from mine. Once again I felt as if I were a snake rising from the basket to the rhythm of her charms, gently swaying. "Surely you are aware of this. Yet you have a plan you must think will work, else why come here."

I forced myself to look away, to break the hypnotic hold. "If you are about to leave, this no longer matters to you."

"They will find me. They will trace me through you."

Light filled the room in that moment and haloed the dark figure who entered. A millisecond too late I recognized the destitute woman on the stairs--still disheveled, but now aiming an energy weapon. I did a tuck and roll and came up with my own weapon. And in the next instant Tsebieh was holding the pistol. Five times it bucked in her hand, the reports slamming off the walls as if we were inside a barrel, and the woman spilled back through the doorway.

Leaving me on one knee, on the floor, staring in disbelief at my own empty hand.

The tavern shook, and I knew it was Big Gooey, stomping down the hallway. At the door he paused over the body on the floor, then turned a face like a parboiled walrus on me.

Before he could vent his rage over the violation of his establishment, Tsebieh said, "She tried to protect me, Gooey. She had nothing to do with it. This is something else."

I rose and crept warily to the corpse--bodies, like weapons, are always presumed to be loaded unless you unload them yourself. This one had a crimson quincunx just under the sternum. You could have covered all five dots with a coaster.

On the floor under the woman, a puddle began to form. Its color matched that of the splatters and streaks down the fractured wall opposite the doorway.

"You use hollow points?" said Tsebieh, hushed, as she passed the pistol back to me.

I tucked it under my belt and pulled the jersey over it. "It's not a toy," I said. "And what I do is not a game."

"I think both of you should leave now," said Big Gooey.

*   *   *

As soon as we left the *Tarry A'Dea* it began to rain. Nevernow, the settlement of which the tavern was the centerpiece, consisted of rough dwellings and shops, small irregular gardens, and clusters of orchards managed by an expatriate populace that regarded strangers the way the Cyclops viewed sailors in distress. Shelter was unlikely.

Tsebieh nudged my arm, and gestured toward the distant escarpment southeast of the settlement, a forbidding dark mass whose broad shadow cast by Vanth almost reached us. Nyx, Chthonia's other moon, lurked just below the eastern horizon. When it rose, we would easily be visible, even in the storm, silhouetted against the night like paperboard targets. I was about to set off when

I felt a brief but intense wave of dizziness. When I opened my eyes again [I did not recall having closed them], Tsebieh and I were standing inside a cavern. The burble of an underground stream replaced the hiss of rain. But I could still smell her lilacs.

"I'm impressed," I told her, regaining my equilibrium. Apparently she came here often--the cavern was lit by a charcoal brazier that stood in the middle of the uneven floor. But the air inside the cavern was cool and moist and old, and I began to feel chilled. "What's your range?"

Tsebieh turned away, and seemed to find something on the cavern wall worthy of fierce attention. Her chest heaved in the aftermath of the effort she had just made, and between breaths she gasped, "I'm not going back there."

"I *told* you---"

"You can't get there from here."

She folded her arms and straightened her spine, unyielding as the wall she stared at. Water dripped from my hair down my face and back, and I blinked as if it were tears. With a stark assertion she had dismissed me. Yet I was still here, even if shunned. What was it she wanted to hear from me?

Outside, lightning flashed, and I caught a glimpse of it through the narrow slit off to my left. A malnourished child might slip into the cavern easily enough, but Tsebieh was safe from adult intruders who lacked her teleportation skills. I squeegeed the rain from my hair and went to peer outside. Briefly the sky lit up, revealing massive banks of black cumulus. Grumbling shook the air seconds later.

It looked to be a long storm, and a long night.

Tsebieh had stowed some rations in a small plastic cooler near the brazier. I rummaged around inside it and finally extracted a stalk of something green, and began to munch on it, remotely wondering whether I was devouring one of her long-lost relatives. Suddenly that thought took solid form inside me--I might have violated her personal repository, and not a food bin.

Tsebieh whirled--she'd disclaimed telepathy, so perhaps I'd made a sound, of disgust, annoyance, apology.

Across the cavern our eyes locked, and hers seemed to penetrate to the back of my skull. I felt like the marionette of an absent-minded puppeteer wondering what that wooden cross was doing in his hand. Then time resumed, and I could move the strings. Again Tsebieh turned away, and drifted to a rock ledge beside the underground stream, and sat down. Her demeanor issued an invitation for me to join her there. I did so. Ancient waterflow had worn the ledge smooth, with a shallow depression that fit my sitting contours comfortably. In the stream glinted the silver of quick, tiny fish. They flitted from one spot to another so swiftly that they might have employed the same method of movement as Tsebieh. Like stars they sparkled. And they had no eyes.

For a while we sat in silence, watching the little fish. They swam as if they possessed an innate sense of position relative to their environment, negotiating the channel with an economy of movement, darting hither and yon without collisions. The attraction they held for Tsebieh was perhaps subsensual. And there are many kinds of darkness, and only one of them involves the absence of light.

I was aware of her, sitting there, on many levels. Long ago, confronted by personal disaster, I too might have fled. But I'd received training in the operation of weaponry and the applications of force, and these I'd turned against those who had provoked me. The price on my head was far less than that on hers, but it was enough to warrant---

"She was after *me*," I said, blurting the realization as it arrived. The fish scattered briefly at the sound of my voice.

Tsebieh was trailing her fingers in the silver water, creating little eddies in which hopeful silver wraiths searched for food, her silver eyes now on me. The force of her persona came not from this world. Like some ancient queen, half leader, half temptress, she cast out her aura and netted me. Had I been encased in stone, I could not have been more immobilized. And she still smelled like lilacs.

The susurrus of her voice might have hypnotized a predator. "Not, perhaps, for what you think. You *are* the woman called Loba?"

My throat tightened. How could my purpose have been known in advance? "Among other things."

"May I know your true name?"

"Emer McClafferty."

"Emer, yes--the great love of Cuchulainn, faithful to the last, despite his many infidelities. Tell me, Emer, what are you faithful *to*?"

Of their own accord, my fists clenched to stone. A desiccating, pungent stench reached the nostrils of my memory--burnt hair and bones, lingering long after the event. Charred framework like skeletons. Leafless trees from an early Van Gogh sketch. With a mighty effort I turned that page.

"You want me to distill a philosophy of twenty words in ten seconds from three decades of experience. I won't even try."

"There are bad people out there," Tsebieh said quietly, succinctly. "And you kill them."

"That's one level of definition."

I thought I knew what was coming next: the tired, specious argument that a killer of killers was morally no better than those she killed. But history has amply demonstrated [though few have learned the lesson] that only dead "bad people" harm no one. Morality be damned, someone has to stop them from harming others. Why not me?

But recently I'd retired from contract work. Of late it had grown tedious, and so I'd opted for voluntary assignments--such as this one.

"And the corporations will not intervene," Tsebieh whispered. "No matter what the harm done, the corporations merely cluck and tisk and then find a way to profit by it." Abruptly she scrambled to her feet and strode away, toward the narrow opening, once again illuminated by the charged black clouds. The glow from outside swirled around her like a creek flowing past a boulder, and cast her in pale silver and shadow as she stood hugging herself, though the warmth from the brazier now filled the chamber.

We'd entered a time of darkness, the interruptive light dangerous. The storm raged as if against her universe, but within the chamber, inside her impregnable fortress, she was safe. She might retreat here from all save her conscience. I'd heard the undertones earlier, in her voice. To deprive GenTail of the ultimate toy...but could it be done?

I could not know Tsebieh's thoughts. Perhaps memories flashed before her, and she was reviewing them for inspiration, for guidance. Of a sentient species, she'd begun life as a reject: a clone no longer needed to provide vital organs to its primary. They'd allowed her to flatline in the repository, and stored her for general harvest, until GenTail purchased the rights to her DNA, as it had done at the commencement of so many other experiments. Revived in GenTail's own concept of image and likeness, they'd spliced into her selected characteristics of cheetah, Polychaeta, and spinach. And other things. Given sunlight, she could never starve--the chlorophyll in her skin would activate if hunger grew extreme. She might adapt to cold by hibernating. And her feline quickness served her well in defense.

But the feline in her also rejected the docility GenTail required of her. Tsebieh came to brook no more experiments, no more alterations. No longer would she submit herself--*the* cardinal sin in the eyes of those who regarded themselves as in authority. The fates thrust the necessity of escape upon her, and she created the opportunity she needed, taking with her the genetic imprints for telekinesis. She was the only one of her kind, if GenTail was to be believed.

And I believed them in this instance. Tsebieh had been their prototype. Forgotten, unwanted, the GenTail technicians might do with her as they wished, and if the experiments ran awry, they might with impunity convert her to so much dust. But she had escaped before they'd conducted sufficient tests, and they were reluctant to alter another being until the test results confirmed their hypotheses.

I might confirm them: I'd witnessed the disappearance of the *gretel* and of herself. But nobody was going to ask me.

Reluctant, was GenTail...but not unwilling. The longer Tsebieh stayed away, the safer she was. There was no shortage of subjects on whom to conduct experiments, and sooner or later the testing would resume. Unless someone prevented that continuation.

Unless someone stopped them.

And there was only one way to do that.

In the shadows by the wall, to one side of the narrow entrance, Tsebieh turned back around. Eyes like freshly stamped coins gazed through mine to the back of my skull. *I don't read minds*, she had asserted in the booth, but I could feel her inside me, rummaging around. Again I asked myself: what was it she wanted to hear from me?

Across the floor of the cavern she drifted, slowing as she drew up to me. I'd not been aware of her height until this moment--her eyes, on a level with mine now, bored into me. I could see my reflection in them. And still I smelled the lilacs.

"If you should obtain this genetic program for telepathy," she asked, "this Teleos Splice, what do you propose to do with it?"

I shrugged one shoulder. "Destroy it somehow."

"Not sell it to the highest bidder? Not attempt to profit by your theft?"

"Is that what you think of me?"

Her hand grasped my arm. "Who are you working for? At least tell me that much."

"In this instance I am self-employed."

"Altruistic? A hardened killer with a soft spot? You, Loba?"

"Call me Emer," I told her. "I prefer that. I have my reasons."

Slowly she nodded, to herself, as if she had confirmed a suspicion. "I think I see. Your one good deed. Very well: what computer skills have you, that you might attempt entry?"

"None that are unusual."

Tsebieh threw up her hands in exasperation. "Then *how*---?"

I told her.

Her voice came out between a gasp and a hush. "I never thought of that."

*   *   *

Although Tsebieh continued to hint at misgivings about the project, the subtle conception of my plan cheered her somewhat during the Track to Mendellia, the aptly-named planet on which the headquarters and laboratories of Genetic Detailing were located. Even so, it was a rough three hours. Confined inside my *Tisiphone*, she became a pacer stalking the gangway between bridge and galley, while I dozed. From time to time there came a clattering from the galley, a rattle of utensils and containers, after which she would emerge porting small plates heaped with crackers and spreads. She munched nervously and sloppily, brushing crumbs from her cammies, and spoke little until we had drawn to within half an hour of arrival.

"Tisiphone?" she said, finally alighting on the starboard captain's chair. "That sounds Greek. Not one of the Fates, surely." She shook her head once, as if debating with herself. With the movement, the overhead illuminative panels gave her short chestnut hair an iridescent sheen. "Furies, perhaps?"

Early in my career I'd succumbed to a maudlin impulse and so christened my 'skip, a blatant advertisement of my occupation and my purpose in life. I'd even dubbed my 'skip's computer Alecto, and had thought of adopting Megaera as a professional name. But I had sobered, and the silly sentimental gestures passed deservedly by the wayside. I'd retained the 'skip's name because it was familiar. Because, in some ways, the 'skip herself was a familiar.

"She was the 'Avenger of Murder,'" I told Tsebieh.

She was silent for a moment. Then: "Someone was taken from you."

The ingenuous statement struck me like a mallet. I busied my hands with the intercom toggles, with a crease in my black denims, with a lock of loose hair. And all the while, Tsebieh allowed me my diversions, waiting patiently for her response.

After my two years at Corporate Security Academy and a year of the usual low-profile security and investigative assignments while I got my professional bearings, I'd taken a brief furlough back to the village of my youth. It wasn't there. They'd razed it. Killed the inhabitants, torched the buildings and the orchards and the fields, plowed everything under. Parents, friends, first loves, even the two stray dogs I'd fed nightly from the back porch despite Mom's admonitions. All gone. The land was scheduled for development...

I checked the virtual distance indicator. Ten minutes to deTrack, fifteen to destination. There was enough time to remember. *Damn Tsebieh, anyway.* But the malediction was unfair. The memories were hardly her fault...

And as I stood on the spot of the village square, I caught whiffs of what had happened. My hair had gotten too close to a campfire once, when I was a child. The stench surrounding me was like that, only a thousand times more powerful. A thousand villagers, counting the livestock. All gone. Because someone had the power to erase them. Because the land was scheduled for development.

My voice was just audible over the memories. "It was long ago and far away, Tsebieh."

"Now there are things wrong which must be put right, is that it?"

I felt a growl catch in my throat. "Is everything so goddamn simple for you? Kill bad people? Right wrongs?"

Tsebieh did not respond to the jab. Seven minutes to deTrack. The extreme port side of the instrumentation console houses several bits of non-standard instrumentation that would probably violate the 'skip's warranty, if discovered...if the *Tisiphone* had a warranty. I flipped a toggle and gave us a new transponder identity-- one that would, I hoped, deflect suspicion from our arrival.

"I won't justify what I do with a platitude, Tsebieh," I said at last. "In the beginning, no, I was...enraged and outraged. I lashed out at the innocent and guilty alike, Tsebieh. Sometimes I had a contract...sometimes not. I wanted justice...I wanted balance for my loss. But Space denies us that expectation. The vast distances preclude effective law enforcement. Oh, maybe here and there local laws apply. But nobody was going to call the murderers of my village to account."

"So you held them accountable."

How could she know precisely which ghost to confront me with, *how*?

"I did nothing of the sort. I have no idea who destroyed Liffee--my village. In time, Agriculture Corporation built and operated banks of storage bins there--so it might have been AgCor Security who 'cleared' the land for this...or it might have been some other corporation. It hardly matters, now."

The *Tisiphone* shuddered briefly, and we deTracked. The stars returned. And 10,000 kilometers ahead hung the mottled blue-green and brown orb of Mendellia. We were visible to their sensors, to their security satellites.

"I changed nothing, Tsebieh," I continued, talking more now to relieve my tension. It occurred to me that I'd spoken more words with her than with any other person in the past ten years. Why the talking jag? Because she listened? "In fact, some of those killings created job openings desired and paid for by other corporate personnel. In fulfilling my contracts, I was doing them favors. I solved nothing. I changed nothing."

"You might have run away," Tsebieh pointed out. "If you can't change it, then get as far away as you can and hope they don't find you."

"What you did."

"But you found me."

I shrugged. "You made it easy. You stayed on Chthonia. You grew roots. That's one reason we might succeed here. Corporations are not mobile entities. They can be found."

She swiveled the chair to face me. "Why, Emer, is that a note of wistfulness I detect?"

"Go to hell." I made a face, at her and at the universe in general. "I can't afford the vulnerability of roots...but yes, if you must know, *yes*, I'd love to have at least a *pied a terre*. At least that."

"As would I," she whispered. "Roots...a place to return to."

"They tend to burn those. Or haven't you noticed?"

And her response was lost when the port communications monitor hissed and a red light on the console began to blink. Someone wanted to talk with us. I heard Tsebieh swallow hard. My own heart was a stone, sinking. I keyed the XMIT, and the hard, stern face of a young man appeared in the monitor.

"Identification and purpose?" Clearly he was a man of few words. He favored a bristle cut for his light brown hair, and his eyes, of the same color, lacked depth. The ideal employee--one day to be bred by GenTail, if the experiments on Tsebieh should prove successful.

"Captain Stahl of Corporate Security, aboard the *Sternweg*," I said. "My aide, Corporal Jensen. We're here for business and pleasure. I wish to see your commanding officer, Captain Bogaty, about...some security matters. Also, my aide and I wish to go fishing."

"Stand by, sir." The monitor blanked.

Tsebieh hissed. "Are you---?" she began, but obeyed the chop of my hand, cutting her off while I flipped the Mute toggle. "*Are you out of your mind?*"

"Probably. Tsebieh, I have several 'borrowed' transponder programs. I know Captain Stahl...enough to know that Bogaty has heard of her. You, I made up...nobody's going to check on the aide. It's the day shift down there; Bogaty will be busy with normal routines. We'll have a couple hours of *unsupervised* visit. Understand?"

"That may not be enough---"

"Hush," I snapped, as the monitor reactivated. The man of few words had a few more for us. The Captain would see us at the end of the duty day, in three hours. We had a room in the Bachelor Officers' Quarters, behind which we might downdock the *Sternweg*, and permission to fish the lake half a kilometer to the south. We'd have to provide our own tackle, and our own flatbottom, or fish from the shore.

"You are also instructed to avoid downdocking within

half a kilometer of the galleon *Bremerhaven* while it discharges cargo," he said. End transmission.

I set the *Tisiphone* to autodock and pocked a knuckle on the point of Tsebieh's shoulder for attention. "I've cammie CorpSec uniforms stowed aft. We should change."

"We're not going fishing?" She got up and followed me to the stateroom. "The lake is closer to the GenTail R&D Labs."

"Low hatchway, watch your head." I ducked inside and made for a stack of bins set against the bulkhead next to the bunk berths, and drew open a drawer. "I'd prefer we remain close to the *Tisiphone*, if not aboard her," I said, tossing her a folded set of CorpSec cammies and a set of corporal's pips. "If we do have to be seen, I want us to blend."

Fortunately Tsebieh and I were almost of a size. She sat down on the lower berth and began to unlace her boots while I laid out a uniform for myself on the upper. It was impossible not to notice that she still smelled of lilacs, not to be aware that she was doffing her clothes. I had not prepared for the sheer impact of that awareness. I felt as if I'd just walked into a stanchion I'd not seen.

I backed away from the berths. Already she was naked save the undies, and was about to climb into the trousers. "Tsebieh..."

One leg in, one leg out, she looked up. Her "Oh" was barely audible. I watched her chest rise and fall, ever so slowly, with a time-weary sigh, not quite of exasperation, not quite of regret, as she straightened to face me, arms at her sides, defenseless. "It's the lilacs," she whispered. "I'm...sorry, I cannot turn them off. But...the attraction you feel for me is only physical. If that helps," she finished lamely.

My throat felt parched, as if by desert air. "A lot of relationships begin that way."

A light impact trembled the *Tisiphone*, bringing her to ground and the two of us back to our purpose. We had arrived. Tsebieh turned away from me and resumed dressing, as did I, and we spoke of this no more.

* * *

The GenTail R&D Labs were located not merely on the other side of the lake, but some eleven kilometers under it, encased in continental granite and virtually indestructible alloy. To physical, electronic, and energy field probes the Labs were opaque and impenetrable, but the encasement was as nothing to someone of Tsebieh's telekinetic abilities. But in the euphoria of having persuaded her to assist me on this self-imposed contract, I'd neglected to determine the parameters of her abilities. I'd supposed that distance was irrelevant--and then she had stipulated that her type of telekinesis needed to be performed from spot to spot on the same planet. That obstacle had been overcome with our arrival on Mendellia.

Mass imposed certain limitations of its own. I hadn't expected her to move an entire planet, or even a continent--merely myself, all 178 centimenters and seventy seven kilograms of me. It seemed simple enough.

But Tsebieh sat down on the lower berth, and shook her head. "You are hardly a bowl of *gretel*, Emer. Think of it this way: you exert your muscles in moving an object in standard gravity. The telekinetic neural module in the brain is not a muscle, of course, but the principle is similar. The more massive the object, the greater the strain, whether physical or telekinetic. Worse, if the object is sufficiently massive, you could strain a muscle, rupture a tendon, tear a ligament. The brain can suffer analogous injuries."

I stared at her. "You mean you *can't* do this, after all?"

"I do not mean to disappoint you, Emer. I have some idea of what this project means to you."

I turned away, walked to the bulkhead, and kicked it. A low *gong* resonated throughout the *Tisiphone*. "Do you really? And what do you think that is?"

Her voice was just audible over the echo. "Redemption."

I barked a laugh. "For what?"

"Your life. Your career."

Her stab was accurate--only partly so, but enough to sting. It was an effort to face her, to meet her eyes with mine. "I regret nothing, Tsebieh, except the lost opportunities to do something positive, something constructive. My anger got in my way. But not this time."

"Tell me more," she urged.

"We haven't time for this right now, remember?"

"Tell me more."

I kicked the bulkhead again, and leaned against it, arms folded. My eyes felt hot now. I spoke in a voice not mine, of thoughts only partially assembled and forced prematurely into the light of analysis. "Very well. There are always people who fight back, who do not care for what they regard as senseless rules imposed upon them. Some of these people are malevolent, that's true enough. But others simply want to be left alone to live their lives, make their mistakes, indulge themselves as they choose, generally without harming others. You find them in many places, Tsebieh...on planets like Chthonia, and in places like the *Tarry A'Dea*. It's not easy, but even now anyone who truly wants to and is determined to do so can opt for freedom by escaping to the Fringes...to the regions where Corporate control is negligible at best. As the Corporations expand, so do the Fringes...and there will always be Fringes. There will always be a place for the likes of you and me to flee to, to live.

"Or so I had supposed. But the Teleos Splice, in time, can destroy the Fringes. It is the ultimate in social and economic control. It can be used to compel *everyone*, no matter how distant, to operate on the same frequency, so to speak. The Fringes will die of neglect; eventually no one will *want* to flee there. Everyone will be doing whatever they are told to do, *forever*. That is what the Teleos Splice makes possible, Tsebieh. We will all think the same thoughts, *forever*. We will think what they tell us to think, do what they tell us to do, buy what they tell us to buy, love and hate what they tell us to love and hate. Those who are in charge, they've been doing that to us for millennia, in one way or another, but there was always somewhere else to go: new lands, new continents, the New World, the Solar planets--but now, once the Teleos Splice is perfected, they can *enforce* their uniformity of thought, of belief, of behavior. They can compel orthodoxy. I want no part of that society, of that universe.

Now *please*, get me inside there and let me do what I came here to do."

Tsebieh did not move from the bed, nor did she lift her gaze from the floor. "So this is personal, for you," she said quietly. "It is not altruism which impels you. This is a selfish act."

I shrugged. "So it's a selfish act."

Tsebieh's voice dropped to a whisper, the eye of the storm. "Everything they did to me, they said it was for my own good."

"Tsebieh..."

Slowly she lifted her face. In the dim light of the stateroom her skin took on an odd reseda glow, powered as if by some internal source, and her eyes shone silver at me. She did not speak of the unimaginable horrors of having her thinking processes experimented upon, of undergoing compulsory alterations in the very core structure of her being, of her spirit, of her soul. She spoke only of the interior of the R&D lab. The lack of inflection in her voice emphasized her furious control over the lightning and thunder behind it.

"The only room of interest is the computer room itself," she said, and I strained to listen, to catch her words. "Security is less than you'd expect. Because unauthorized entry is impossible, no sensors are emplaced. However, I cannot know the effect of telekinetic penetration of the dampening field that surrounds the room. It is possible that porting you through it will raise an alarm. If that should happen, you will have from five to eight minutes to complete your task--the time it takes for an individual who is authorized entry to reach the entrance to the computer room, confirm his or her identity, and enable the doors open. It is also possible that your body might interrupt various signals. The computer is not hardwired in any way. Exchange of information is done through variable-frequency microwaves--another reason why the computer is unhackable."

I strapped on my shoulder rig, and verified the full load in my pistol. "I'll use the commo tube to keep you advised of my progress," I told her. "You can transmit from the bridge comm."

Tsebieh shook her head. "The transmission might be detected, and certainly the dampening field will kill it."

"Then how---?"

Like this, Emer. They can't detect this, yet.

My knees buckled. "I thought you said you can't read minds."

Not can't. Don't.

"They experimented with the Teleos Splice on you, then?"

But they've no idea how successful it was.

I shoved aside a billion questions and instead drew a deep breath, as if preparing to dive under water. "I'm ready."

A wall of dizziness slugged me like a crashing wave in a storm, inundating me. Pressure on my chest inhibited my breathing. In its wake I was aware of a hard surface under my boots. I could barely stand. I braced my arms on top of something--a desk or table--and waited until the universe decided to hold still again. My pounding heart continued to flood adrenalin throughout my body. I was as ready for anything, including my own death, as I would ever be.

Balance returned, and in the darkness I switched on the pencil beam on my cap and scanned about. I was standing inside a cube approximately three meters on a side, beside another cube perhaps one meter on a side that rested on the floor--the computer. This face of its cowling was blank, so I walked around it until I came to the maintenance door Tsebieh had assured me would be there. It felt made of structural plastic, and slid open to the left at my touch. To a computer curious about my identity, I might have been a systems engineer.

"Tsebieh."

Right here, Emer.

Her "voice" sounded strained. "What's wrong?" I asked her.

Inside to the right is a small control panel. Look for Release, or Cowling Release, and enable it.

I scanned the interior of the main computer. I saw a mass of compact technology and heard some faint whirring. I saw nothing that might indicate a control panel.

Tsebieh's silence was long enough to make my heart begin to stutter. Something was not as she had expected, or had given me to expect...but what?

Look again. It has to be there.

"I don't see it."

Omigod. Oh, God...

My mind clenched like a fist--the effect of Tsebieh's panic. Instinctively my hand dipped to the weapon under my arm and grasped the butt. The cold metal comforted me only a little. If Tsebieh lost the telekinetic connection with me, I was trapped beyond rescue. With luck I might dispatch one security guard per round when they came for me, as inevitably they would. I felt reasonably certain that GenTail had far more security guards than I had bullets.

"Tsebieh!"

I can't...

"We're running out of time, Tsebieh."

But you promised me...you assured me...omigod...

"Tsebieh! What should I do?"

I thought I heard her scream, the shriek of an eagle mortally wounded. It might have been my imagination. Then a light puff of air buffeted my right side, and I caught a hint of lilacs. Her shoulder brushed mine as she leaned forward, bracing her arms on the cowling. She was making little sounds with each rapid respiration--*uh ugh uh ugh*--as if she were suffering from an acute coronary disturbance. In the light of the pencil beam she turned horror-filled silver eyes toward me. She looked on the verge of passing out. I tried to steady her, but she drew from a reservoir of strength and shrugged violently away.

Damn you, Emer.

"Tsebieh---"

"Don't talk!" she hissed. "Shut up shut up shut up."

"It's a blown mission," I said. "Let's just---"

The wrath of her "No!" reverberated in the small room like a thunderclap. Snatching my pencil beam, she peered into the opening, studying the layout, comparing what she saw with what she remembered, the way old friends do who've not seen each other for years. "You're right," she said dully. "It's not there." She aimed the beam at the floor and finally scuffed her boot at some object there. With a little whimper she sat down tailor-fashion on the floor, hunched over, mewling.

"Tsebieh?"

The beam trembled in her hand. She brought it to bear on a corner of the cowling, where it joined the floor.

"They've bolted it down," she whispered.

"Then we can't move it," I said. "We can't steal the whole fucking computer. The mission is a scrub. Let's---"

"Shut up. I can't think." Tsebieh pressed fists to her head as if to compel thought by the pressure of her terror, and began to rock back and forth the way autistic children do, listening to their own music. She was withdrawing into her own black depths, and there was nothing I might do for her.

On the other hand, I wasn't going anywhere without her. I knelt down and slipped an arm around her shoulders. She stiffened at the contact, but otherwise did not resist. The scent of lilacs was overpowering. "If we leave now," I said softly, "we can come back. If they come here and catch us, we lose that option."

Tsebieh continued to rock against me, making little mewling noises, as if the spirit of her no longer inhabited her body. I heard something squeak and scrape, and aimed the pencil beam in that general direction.

The bolt on the flange at the right corner of the cowling had emerged a full two centimeters from the floor, and ever so slowly was turning.

Another faint sound reached my ears, as if a small terrestrial creature were crawling through dry leaves-- against the sleeves of my cammies the fine hairs on my forearms were coming erect. I stood as paralyzed as a bird before a snake, watching the dark magic unfold. The bolt twisted round and round, slowly, inexorably, emerging, another centimeter and another. Tsebieh was gasping for air. The light from the pencil beam reflected back at me from the perspiration on her pale forehead. Eyes squeezed shut, she was focusing all of her unique energies on the task at hand. Beads of water dripped from her nose, the point of her chin. And finally I heard a dull *clunk* as the bolt fell free.

Every evil thing they had done to her for her own good, she was turning against them.

"That's one," she whispered, breathless.

Behind me the next bolt protested its astral extraction. If one could summon the dead, they might make that sound as they emerged from the floor. I felt the urge to light a candle. But the pencil beam was sufficient unto the darkness.

A *clunk*, followed at a longer interval by another. Tsebieh was leaning against the cowling, her breathing shallow, face chalky. She peered up at me through half-lidded eyes.

"Don't try to stop me, Emer..."

I knelt down again. "But you're dying."

Drained of her physical strength by the effort she had put forth, Tsebien pushed against me ineffectually. "One more, Emer. Then we can take this with us."

I stood up, and put my weight against the cowling, testing its resistance. "With only one to secure it, I should be able to snap the flange---"

"Not structural plastic. And don't speak, please."

Enfeebled and wan, Tsebieh returned to her task. Unable to assist, I found that I could not bear to watch her exertions and the effects they had on her. By the time I reached the far corner of the cowling, the bolt securing the flange was all but free. But at what cost? And what might we accomplish now?

"Tsebieh?"

"Your concept," she gasped. "My purpose."

I dashed around the corner, fearing the worst, but she had managed to pull herself erect, albeit on unsteady legs. I gave her a once-over with the pencil beam. Many in the past I had killed, or watched die, enough to recognize that she was on the verge. Her death was a consequence I could not permit. If someone was meant to die in this venture, it should be me. I had initiated it; I was responsible.

But Tsebieh was having none of it. "Ready, Emer?"

"Damn it, Tsebieh, at least pause for breath!"

She shook her head once, emphatically, the only gesture she had the strength to make, and slumped over the top of the cowling. Before I could protest, darkness buffeted me, a sensation rather different from my telekinetic journey into the computer room. If she expired while I was in transit, would I be condemned to walk a night like Hamlet's father, but in a night that existed for myself alone? Would I ever catch the scent of lilacs again?

*   *   *

I came to in a darkness that seemed to confirm the worst of my fears and expectations. The floor chilled me through the cammie fabric, and some massive object with canvas straps supported me. My fingers crept along them to the buckles. In my other hand I still grasped the pencil beam. I had to will myself to raise it and enable the light.

I was not aboard the *Tisiphone*.

Around me stood stacks of cargo crates, secured to the bulkheads as proof against zero-gee. The stencils indicated a wide range of disparate products, the sort of inventory one might find in a delivery craft. Scanning for Tsebieh, I gave them only token attention. Belatedly it occurred to me to hail her through my thoughts. But she did not respond. My heart sank.

Although the crates were secured, I was not, but the craft was still bound by the gravity of Mendellia. I climbed to my feet and waited until the waves of unsteadiness abated before panning the beam around the cargo bay. A lump in the shadows against the adjacent bulkhead looked dishearteningly familiar. I dashed to it, to the echoes of my footfalls on the deck, and fell to my knees beside her. She was barely conscious. I folded my legs under to create a lap, and cradled her head on it. Silver eyes shone up at me.

"You were the target, Emer," Tsebieh whispered hoarsely, "and not myself."

What the hell are you talking about? Aloud I added, "Huh?"

"GenTail must have suspected you had a purpose for me. You had to be stopped. But of course they wanted me alive."

The woman who intruded on us in the Tarry A'Dea?

"They knew we might be coming here, Emer. But they did not expect...what we did."

And what did we do, Tsebieh? Where is the computer?

"I put it aboard the *Tisiphone*. I enabled the automatic pilot after 'creating' a few astrogational glitches. The course will accidentally take the cruiser into the Mendellian star, which it should be reaching...about now."

They're following it? GenTail is chasing it?

Tsebieh's head rocked in my lap. "No...monitoring only. It's all over for them...for now. We deprived them of much more than just the Teleos Splice. Everything they had done, all their records of all their projects, were stored in that invulnerable and impregnable computer. They have decades of work to recreate, perhaps even a century of it. We hurt them beyond their ability to calculate. Fortunately for you, they'll believe you dead aboard the *Tisiphone*."

"*You* hurt them, Tsebieh," I said.

"Yes...yes, I did, didn't I?" The deck under us trembled gently, and I knew the cargo craft--the *Bremerhaven*, I remembered--was Tracking into a position around Mendellia preparatory to departure for the next leg of its journey. Tsebieh seemed to be listening to other voices. "They've cleared us for departure," she said at last. I felt a momentary queasiness as zero gee took effect. "I rather thought they would. According to the captain, your next port of call will be Zlatka."

"*Our* next port of call, you mean."

"Someone like you can reach the Fringes easily enough from there."

"Tsebieh---"

"Don't talk. And do not weep."

I drew a wrist across my eyes. "I'm not crying. The air in here is dry."

"You'll have to disappear for a while, Emer."

"Tsebieh, no." I leaned over her, and embraced her, to hold her there. But I could not restrain the part of her that would leave.

"Emer..."

"Right here, Tsebieh."

"Aboard the *Tisiphone*...when we changed clothing. You would have kissed me?"

"More than kissed."

"Kiss me now."

Lips tasting of tears are always best for kissing. Despite her condition, her mouth was wet and inviting, and I longed to linger there forever. But the contact could not endure. And I felt a sharp pain in my lower lip—she had bitten me.

Confused and a little frightened, I drew my face from hers to stare down at her. Her lips were stained with my blood. "Tsebieh, what was that for?"

But the scent of lilacs had faded, and she was gone.

* * *

Five years passed before I dared return to Chthonia. The escarpment southeast of Nevernow had changed little, although the terrain in front of it was less than familiar. It had rained the night Tsebieh and I had fled to the safety of her cavern, and it had rained the night I buried her on the gentle slope in front of the entrance. It had still been raining when I slipped into the *Tarry A'Dea* to arrange discreet transportation elsewhere.

The Chthonian sun shone brightly these days of late spring, but I was shaded where I sat reading meditative poetry on the grass under the tree that had grown so swiftly on the slope near the entrance to the cavern. A low tray beside me supported a tall glass of gin and tonic and a small bowl of nuts and dried fruit. From time to time I glanced at the tree, both in reverie and in awe. The trunk seemed sturdy enough...

The trunk seemed sturdy enough, but the elongated growth within it had now spread the bark almost to the bursting point. I turned a page, and put a finger to the scar on my lower lip, and wondered whether our daughter would have eyes of silver.

The Free Zone
Barbara Candiotti

Bryce stood atop a ridge of dunes overlooking a crescent-moon-shaped lake. It was morning, and a dirty apricot haze hung in the air. He licked his dry, chapped lips and ignored the throbbing, dull ache behind his eyes. He had run out of water twenty-some hours ago. Bryce knew the lake was toxic but had one purifying tab left and hoped it would be enough to get him to the Free Zone.

He had entered this desert region two days ago. The convex-shaped lake was the landmark he had been looking for. From here, the Free Zone was only a week's journey away. Bryce scanned the sun-bleached lakeshore filled with giant boulders of broken concrete and rusted rebar. Bird carcasses and animal bones added organic texture - but no humans or wildlife were visible. He trained his binocs on the lake, mesmerized by the rhythmic motion of the waves. The water's movement stirred his subconscious, allowing a visceral memory to flood in - sailing on a pristine lake under an azure sky with his beautiful wife. The memory bent Bryce over with grief - then a surge of anger.

"Goddamn, AI, Goddamn AI!" He spit on the sand.

Bryce slowly straightened up his right hand, instinctively holding his right side. He felt the prominent bones of his lower ribcage and the scar over the spot where his kidney should be.

Why didn't they kill me and take both my kidneys? Why take only one? What could a machine want with a human kidney? He traced the uneven scar with his finger.

Bryce was a former soldier in the unsuccessful war against the rise of sentient AI. He had lost his wife and home in the hostilities. After the war, the prevailing AI designated an undeveloped region for humans to live technology-free. They called it the "Free Zone" and instructed the remaining people to migrate there.

Bryce thought about the cabin he would build in the Free Zone, similar to the rustic hunting cabin he had helped his father build as a teenager. The early American Pioneers were skilled hunters, trappers, farmers, and carpenters. I can do what they did and more, he thought.

Out of the side of his right eye, he caught movement. A swarm of black dots headed his way. "CRAP!" he said as he dove face down into the broiling dunes. He wiggled and buried his body as much as possible, letting the loose sand envelop him. He hoped the drones wouldn't detect his thermal signature in the hot sand. He held his breath as the drone swarm flew past him. Their high-pitched whine sent a chill down his back.

"Tin-can killer bees," he exhaled.

Bryce slowly stood and scuttled down the dunes toward the lake. He was halfway between the dunes and the lakeshore when he heard the high-pitched whine again. Before he could dive for cover, a hive of ten glinting obsidian drones surrounded him. Some bristled with razor-sharp instruments, while others bore drills and saws.

A surgical field squad, he thought as beads of sweat erupted on his forehead and upper lip.

The scan, a low resonant oscillating wave, rippled through him stinging his skin and entrails, leaving him faint and his ears ringing.

"Your body is dehydrated," the closest drone said in a toneless metallic voice.

"No shit, and I could use a bite to eat, too!"

The drone ignored him.

"Heart excellent, check
Liver average, check
Lungs good, check
Eyes excellent, check
Hands and face good, check
One kidney good, check."

The drone paused, emitted a click-beep, then said, "You will die in approximately fifty-one hours and thirty seconds unless your body receives hydration. You desire to reach the Free Zone."

"Good guess, Sherlock!"

Click-beep, pause...,

"The Free Zone is not...," click-beep, "the Free Zone is not...,"

"What?" Bryce narrowed his eyes at the drone. "The Free Zone is not - WHAT?"

"Never mind, we will help you."

"Oh yeah? What will it cost me?"

"We require one of your eyes. You can choose which one."

"Why not wait till I'm dead and take all my organs?"

"We prefer your cooperation. In return, you will get enough rations and water to get to the Free Zone."

Bryce's mind whirled. Could he manage without one eye? Yes, but he had bucked intimidation and bullies all his life. Was he going to acquiesce this close to the Free Zone?

"SHHH-CRAAAAAK!" The lead drone bounced, crackling with static.

The other drones quivered, and their hum ratcheted up an octave higher.

"Stay here! We have detected more humans nearby."

Bryce heard a click, and a sharp sting hit the back of his neck. His hand shot up to feel a geo-tag burrow under his skin, mimicking a hungry tick.

"Bastards!"

The drones roared off at high speed.

Bryce turned in a circle looking for cover, anything to escape an eye extraction. He noticed a change in the curvature of the dunes about fifty yards to his left. There appeared to be a hint of a trail and a separation in the dunes as they hugged the lake. He sprinted toward the faint path. Once he passed through the split in the dunes, he found himself at the bottom of a narrow canyon. The canyon was about eight feet wide, with walls on either side that rose ten to twenty feet above his head. The air was noticeably cooler with a welcome hint of dampness.

Bryce paused to lean against the cool rock wall to catch his breath.

This wash should lead to fresh water. Will I be able

to find it? Can I escape the black drones? He wondered.

Fatigue engulfed him. He closed his eyes.

I just need some rest and clean water. I can make it.

A small red drone was hovering at eye level when he opened his eyes. It had no rotor blades and sounded like a hair dryer.

That's an ion-powered drone! He raised his eyebrows in surprise. Hi-tech advanced shit!

Then Bryce noticed the menacing cannon mounted under the square body of the drone. A keen spear tip protruding from it. He surmised it was a dart gun tipped with a paralyzing agent. He pressed his back into the wall.

"What do you want?" he said.

A sudden scan sliced through him - a shock of arctic cold, followed by the sensation of freezing mist. He gasped and wiped droplets of water from his face. It was as if he had entered a walk-in freezer and exited in an ice fog.

"That should perk you up," a melodious female voice said.

"What kind of scan was that?" Bryce asked, "I feel like a plant spritzed with ice water."

"Excellent observation," the drone replied. "We extracted moisture from this rock corridor and amped it up with our proprietary "Hydro Nano Dust," bestowing you with refreshing micro-hydration."

"Why would you do that?"

"There is something you have that we are interested in. Consider the hydrating scan a gift, a gesture of goodwill."

"I suppose you want an eye, too."

"I see you had a run-in with those crude organ harvesters – a most unpleasant bunch. You were geo-tagged too."

"What's it to you?"

"I'll get to that, but we must get rid of the tag first. Please turn around."

Bryce eyeballed the drone. It was flitting up and down in a threatening holding pattern. The cannon shifted and homed in on his torso with a precision clink sound.

"Turn around now!"

Warily, Bryce closed his eyes and slowly turned around.

He pictured the small cabin he was going to build. It would be tucked under shade trees with a chicken pen in the back and a large garden along the side. He remembered the rumor floating around near the war's end – some AI were helping humans. There was talk of a split in the AI hive mind. Some AI was said to be even giving medical care to humans. However, his captain had always said, "Never trust AI."

This drone seems different, Bryce thought and allowed himself a glimmer of hope.

He felt a needle prick, then heard a harsh, low-pitched hiccupping tone and a tugging pull at his neck.

"Got it," the drone said.

Bryce patted his neck and turned to face the drone. There was a pungent burnt smell in the air, and he could see wisps of smoke.

"Thanks," Bryce said. "Now tell me what you want?"

"The hunter drones are coming!"

When their geo-tags lose signal, they immediately head to the last geo-tag location.

"Quick! Follow me. We need to get to safety."

The drone bounced in agitation, then shot abruptly down the canyon path.

I'll play along. This little drone is sophisticated and seems friendly. Maybe it will help me, Bryce thought.

Bryce sprinted after the drone. The drone took a sharp right and disappeared out of sight. When Bryce made the same turn, he entered an opening in the canyon with very narrow walls forcing him to turn sideways to traverse it. After a few twists and turns, the path came to a dead end. The red drone was nowhere in sight. The dead end was odd - a conical sphere cut in the canyon walls, narrowing to a cylindrical neck above his head.

This shape, it's too precise, he thought.

Bryce turned in a circle spreading his arms out, his fingertips barely touching the walls. A dark ocher light filtered into the space from an opening he could not see.

Feeling like a bug in an Erlenmeyer flask, he turned to flee the way he had come in but tripped and fell to his knees. Bryce tried to get up, but his limbs were leaden, and his mind was groggy. He looked up and saw the red drone emitting a fine mist spray. Then everything went black.

When he woke, he found himself on his back, lying on compacted sand and dirt. It was pitch black. Panicked, he shot up to a sitting position.

Bryce's mind raced. Where am I? What happened?

He quickly assessed his body, patting his arms, legs, and midsection. He had all his limbs. He didn't feel pain or dullness, which he had felt when he woke up missing a kidney.

My eyes! He thought as his hands flew to his eyes. He felt cloth. A piece of rough fabric wound around his head and eyes.

No, please, not my eyes!

He tore away the cloth. Underneath, he felt a bandage across both eyes and faint light filtered through the dressing.

"I can see!" He cried.

Carefully he peeled off the bandage. Where his eyes should have been, he felt hard plastic and metal. He sensed a slight vibration and heard a low hum, and suddenly his mind was flooded with crystal-clear images. He was in a cave. He could see every detail of the rough rock walls down to the tiniest cracks. He turned his head side to side, awed by the vividness of his sight. Yet something wasn't right. Everything had a strange phosphorus-green tint.

That's when he saw the note. A radiant white square of light pinned to his chest. He opened it and began to read:

'Dear Traveler,

As you know, it's a cut-throat world we live in, and unfortunately, human eyes, among other parts, are in high demand. We took yours but have replaced them with our latest synthetic eye technology, which includes a geo-tag.

We know you had high hopes for the Free Zone, but it's different from what you think it is. Sorry to be the bearer of unwelcome news, but the Free Zone is unsafe for humans. It is meant to coalesce humans into an easily accessible area. There are many AI that want to be human. As you would expect, this desire requires lots of body parts. Unlike the hunter drones, we pursue technical challenges for sport, not humans. But alas, we still need to trade for things we require. That is where you come in. Your assignment is to trap humans for us. One human a month starting now. Your geo-tag will be offered to the highest hunter drone bidder if you don't comply.

We expect to find your prey in one month at this location.

Happy Hunting,
-The Red Drone"

Bryce read the note twice, crumpled it into a ball, and threw it on the ground.

That's why they want human body parts, and the Free Zone is nothing more than a holding pen. His stomach clenched, and he doubled over with shock.

"Goddamn AI, Goddamn AI," he slammed his fists into the dirt.

After a while, a sense of eerie calm came over him, and his mind shifted into a crystal-clear focus. A static radio station latching on to a strong signal.

There's got to be a way out of this, he thought.

He felt the exterior of his new eyes - they wrapped around the front of his face, similar to goggles but did not extend to his ears. They had a rubbery feel and were pliable.

They could be cut, he thought as he tapped the frame with his fingertips.

The barest hint of light flickered and danced at the cave's entrance. Bryce watched the shots of light get bigger and bigger, then rose to his feet. He pressed his lips together, squared his shoulders, and then headed toward the illumination.

"Never trust AI," his captain's words echoed in his mind.

One month to figure out how to survive without eyes.

He fingered the knife on his belt.

How I Saved the World and Got Grounded for Six Months
James Rumpel

I was actually hanging pretty close to Riley this round. I've played him in Super Smash Brothers thousands of times and only managed to beat him about ten percent of the time. So, I was elated when he failed to counter my attack and his last character went flying off the screen. That is until I realized that he was sitting motionless on the edge of my bed, a dazed expression on his face. The only other time I had ever seen Riley look that confused was halfway through Mrs. Finkel's Algebra final.

"Are you okay?" I asked. "You can't be that shocked that I beat you?"

He just sat there, staring at me.

"Riley. Say something."

Finally, he spoke. His words came out slow and monotone. "I am not Riley."

I laughed. "Good one. You don't have to pretend to be crazy just because I finally beat you."

He ignored me. "This is not right. I am not where I should be."

"What are you talking about? Your mom gave you permission to spend the night at my house."

Riley stood and walked toward the mirror above my dresser. He stared at his reflection. "I am but a child. How am I supposed to carry out my mission in this body?"

"That's enough, Riley," I muffled my yell. If my parents woke up and found my friend acting like this, they'd think we were on drugs or something. "Quit acting so weird." I was beginning to believe that this wasn't an act. Riley could never have pulled this kind of gag off without breaking into laughter.

Riley turned to me. "Where am I? Who are you?"

"I'm Billy, Billy White. This is my house."

"I mean, what are our current coordinates? I am supposed to be at 45.73 degrees North by negative 93.017 degrees East. There is a city there called St. Paul."

I shrugged. I didn't know the coordinates of my house and I was positive that Riley wouldn't know the coordinates of St. Paul either. "We're about thirty miles from St. Paul. This is Hudson, Wisconsin."

Riley stared at me. He still showed no emotion whatsoever. "You need to take me to the desired coordinates. The address is 215 Kellogg Boulevard, suite 93."

"Cut it out, Riley," I said. I moved toward him and reached to grab him by the shoulders.

In one fluid motion, Riley ducked under my outstretched arms and pulled both my arms behind my back.

"I do not wish to hurt you. I need your assistance. It is a matter of great importance."

Riley could never have pulled off the maneuver he had just completed. I had no idea how it had happened but I was certain that someone or something had taken control of Riley's body.

"Okay, this is just too crazy. Who are you and what have you done to Riley?" I glanced around the room trying to find where I had put my cell phone. "I'm going to call the police."

"Do not alert the authorities. My mission must be kept a secret. The fate of your planet is at stake."

He released his grip on me and I turned to face him. I had a ton of questions but all I could do was sit there and stare at Riley, dumbfounded.

He paused. I suppose he was considering his options. Finally, he continued. "I have been sent from an alien spacecraft in orbit around the planet you call Jupiter. We cannot come any closer to Earth for fear of being discovered. There is an intergalactic terrorist in St. Paul who is going to set off an explosive that is powerful enough to destroy your world. I need to find this terrorist and disarm his weapon as soon as possible. You must take me to St. Paul." When he finished the explanation, Riley sat back down on my bed. He shook his head and tried to suppress a yawn.

"Why would a space terrorist be trying to blow up Earth? What did we do?"

"This creature has threatened to destroy primitive planets until he is given control of a large portion of the galaxy. We cannot allow this to happen."

"But why Earth?" I asked. "You said he's destroying primitive planets."

Riley just stared at me.

I thought about my options. I considered just running from the room and getting away from whatever mysterious being had possessed my friend. I watched for any sign that Riley was still somewhere inside his body. Then I noticed the series of posters I had hanging on my walls. Ironman, Batman, Aaron Rogers, and Wonder Woman all looked back at me. None of them would hesitate when it came to saving the world. I wouldn't either. It was my duty as a citizen of Earth and a member of the Hudson Middle School student council.

"I could wake my dad and he could drive us, but he's not going to believe your story."

"No," replied Riley. "I have already broken protocol by informing you of the situation. We must do this alone and we must start immediately."

"I suppose we could take my sister's car. She doesn't use it because she's off to college. I can't legally drive. I'm only fourteen but Dad's let me back the car into the garage a few times and I drove Ricky Callahan's four-wheeler when we were at boy scout camp. It can't be that hard. It's late at night there won't be many cars on the road."

"We will leave immediately." After a brief pause, Riley added, "It must be late in this body's sleep cycle. It appears to be very low on energy. Where do you keep your energy supplements? I could use a large dose."

"Uh . . . We don't have supplements. We go to sleep when we are tired."

Riley shook his head. "We don't have time for sleep. You must have some sort of supplement that I can use to energize this body."

I thought for a minute. "Well, I guess we've got a twelve-pack of Mountain Dew in the refrigerator in the garage."

***

Sneaking out of the house was no problem and since my sister's car was parked in the driveway, we were able to get away without my parents hearing us, though I did come close to knocking over the mailbox. We live about three miles from the freeway and that first leg of our trip was pretty slow. By now, it was almost 2 in the morning and there was little to no traffic on the road.

Eventually, I started to get the hang of driving and by the time I got to the freeway on-ramp, we were clipping along at a solid 40 miles per hour. We drove in silence. I was concentrating on not crashing. Riley sat beside me, intently scanning my phone and guzzling his third can of Mountain Dew.

The speedometer reading climbed to almost fifty and I finally felt confident enough to start asking some of the thousands of questions welling up inside me.

"If you're an alien, how come you speak English and can read and stuff?"

Without looking up, Riley answered, "I learned enough of your language to complete my mission. Your communication processes are very simple and easy to master."

"If you're so smart, why did they send you to the body of a kid?"

"I have been trying to determine that and have just found the answer. I was supposed to be placed in the body of a police officer near our destination. The address we are heading to contains a locker with everything I need to disable the explosive. I have just searched your internet for information and it appears that the officer I was to occupy was shot and killed at approximately the same moment the transference was to occur. The computer in charge of the transfer had to make an emergency adjustment and send me to this body."

I took my eyes off the road long enough to take a quick look to my right. I'd known Riley for his entire life, I could safely say that his body was not made for confrontation or for being a hero. "Why would it choose Riley?" I refocused on the road as one of the rare other cars on the highway shot past us.

"The algorithm for selection is very complicated. The calibrations must be extremely accurate and the host's brain must have a specific configuration for my consciousness to be implanted. I assume your friend was the closest vessel that matched the calibration specifics. If the transfer had already started when the desired host was killed the computer would not have had sufficient time to redo the calculations and could only send me to the nearest acceptable recipient."

"Well, I don't understand all that, but I can tell you, Riley is not going to be a very good host. He's kind of a nerd . . . and a wimp."

Red and blue flashing lights appeared directly behind our car.

"Damn," I said, "It's the police."

"Don't stop," ordered Riley. "We cannot afford any delay."

"I'm not running from the police," I said as I pulled the car to the side of the road. "I am going to be in enough trouble the way it is."

"I will handle it," said Riley.

We both watched as the police officer made his way to the driver's side of the car. I rolled down the window, fighting back tears.

Before I could say anything, the officer shined his flashlight into the car.

"I pulled you over because you were driving erratically and way below the speed limit. I need to see your license . . ."

Suddenly, Riley burst out of the car and leaped across the hood. With catlike quickness, he swung his leg into the back of the officer's knees. The officer, who was a large man, lost his balance and stumbled forward. Somehow, Riley jumped on his back and put him in some sort of sleeper hold, dragging him to the ground. I had to remind myself that this wasn't the little kid who got cut from the middle school wrestling team because he cried every time Tom Hooperman put him in a half-nelson. My companion wasn't a little boy, he was a trained assassin. The next thing I knew, Riley was back in the seat next to me.

"Go! Drive as fast as you can. We need to get as close to the destination as we can before we abandon the vehicle."

Shaking worse than when I tried to ask Hillary Woodruff to the snowball dance, I obeyed Riley's order. I threw the car into gear and took off. The tires spun and kicked up gravel from the side of the road. Through the rearview mirror, I saw the police officer roll onto his stomach and begin to get up.

Luckily for us, we didn't see any other cars or police vehicles. We made it a couple of more miles before Riley ordered me to pull off the freeway and onto a side street.

He looked up from my phone. "There is a great deal of police activity in the area. They might be looking for us or it may be due to the shooting earlier. Whatever the reason, I will have to proceed on foot. You may remain here. Thank you for your service."

I climbed out of the car as he did. "I'm coming with you. If nothing else I have to make sure Riley is okay. He is going to come back, isn't he?"

Riley was already sprinting down the street faster than I thought he could. I chased after him. "Yes," he called back to me, "he will be returned to his body when the mission is complete."

I wanted to say more but I was already out of breath.

***

I finally caught up to Riley outside the back door of a large office building. He was panting heavily. Each breath he took was accompanied by a loud wheeze.

"Your friend has not kept his body in adequate physical condition," he said between gasps. After a short time, he straightened up and began pressing buttons on a keypad located next to the door. The door clicked and we entered the building.

"Follow me," said Riley, "I need to get some equipment from suite 93."

"How'd you get equipment here," I asked as I followed him into the stairwell.

"A previous agent acquired the necessary materials and constructed the devices I will need. They were placed here in preparation for my mission."

"Why doesn't that agent finish the mission for you?"

"We can only occupy your bodies for a short time before the host is destroyed. That agent was returned to our ship. Also, that agent specializes in procurement and construction. He is not trained in physical combat."

I trudged up eight flights of stairs and found Riley waiting on the landing. He was finishing another can of Mountain Dew.

"I must say, this Mountain Dew does not provide as much energy boost as our supplements but it has a pleasant taste. Also, the bubbles tickle my nose."

Without waiting for me to respond, he opened the ninth-floor access door and took off down the hall. After typing in another code, he entered suite 93.

I watched from the doorway as he went to a file cabinet against the back wall and opened a secret panel. He pulled out a couple of strange-looking devices and a vial of some sort. One of the devices looked like a small plastic water pistol while the other seemed to be nothing more than a metal rod with three balls attached to one end.

I was going to ask what those things were but I didn't get a chance. Riley raced past me and started back down the stairs.

"Hurry," he called, "we must reach the parking garage within eighteen chrono-units."

I had no idea what a chrono-unit was but I followed as quickly as I could.

***

We snuck across the street, ducked behind a recycling bin to avoid a passing squad car, and then raced down the stairs to the bottom level of a large parking ramp.

Riley threw open the door to reveal an empty lot. There were no cars down here, but a homeless man was standing by a cluttered shopping cart. Riley raised his plastic gun and aimed it at the old man.

"Freeze, Amex," shouted Riley.

The homeless man turned to face us, a sneer on his lips. "You're too late."

Suddenly, the man's demeanor changed. The evil smile disappeared and was replaced with a look of utter confusion. His eyes darted all around as if trying to figure out where he was.

"Did the bad guy get away?" I asked.

Riley was already racing toward the shopping cart. He pushed his way past the bum and began tearing through the collection of garbage and bags. "We have to find the explosive so I can disarm it. We don't have much time."

I had no idea what I was looking for but I began opening plastic bags. Inside the first was a collection of rotten banana peels. I quickly closed it and tossed it aside, turning my head to avoid the smell.

"It has to be here somewhere," said Riley as he unrolled a ragged blanket revealing a handgun. He tossed it aside and continued searching. "Amex has to have hidden it somewhere. We're almost out of time."

Then I saw it. "Over there," I shouted as I pointed toward a nearby parking space. "That fancy leather luggage."

Riley was there before I even finished. He unzipped the bag and looked inside. Immediately, he pulled the vial and the strange device from his pocket. He poured whatever was in the vial over the balls attached to the end of the stick.

The three balls started spinning and Riley shoved the contraption inside the suitcase. After a minute, he removed the device and opened the suitcase the rest of the way. "We made it in time," he said. "The neutralizing agent is working perfectly. The explosive is no longer dangerous."

I looked over his shoulder and saw nothing but a

gob of black goo inside the case.

"Thank you," said Riley. "How did you know the explosive was there."

I shrugged. "I just guessed." I pointed at the homeless man who was still standing there watching us, more confused than before. "I figured there was no way he would have expensive luggage like that."

"You have done a great service. You have saved your world."

"But Amex, or whatever you called him got away. I'm guessing he jumped out of that old guy when you were aiming your weapon at him."

Riley nodded. "Yes," he said. "I'm afraid he was able to transfer before I could stop him. In all likelihood, he has returned to his ship. He is still a threat to this world and many others. However, we were able to save your planet this time."

The sound of sirens interrupted any further conversation. I turned to see two police cars come down the ramp and stop in front of the homeless man. The poor fellow didn't even move.

A pair of officers jumped out of each car; weapons drawn.

"You're going to help me get out of this mess, aren't you?" I asked.

Riley only stared at me. "Where am I? What's going on?"

***

They read us our rights and made us stand against the wall. Two officers held us at gunpoint as they waited for the policeman Riley had assaulted on the highway to show up and make a positive identification. The homeless man was also taken into custody, probably for the murder of the policeman earlier that night.

Riley tried to ask what had happened, but they wouldn't allow us to speak to each other.

I considered telling them everything. I could explain how Riley had been possessed and how I had helped an alien operative stop an intergalactic terrorist from blowing up the Earth but I knew no one would believe me any more than Mrs. Finkel believed my most recent explanation for not completing an assignment. Maybe when they brought my father to see me in jail, I could try to tell him. That is if he didn't disown me.

Nearly fifteen minutes passed before another police car arrived carrying the officer Riley had disabled. He took one look at Riley and me and nodded his head.

"Yup, that's them."

One of the other officers chuckled loudly. "You got your butt handed to you by those two?"

"The report says it was only one of them," added another policeman, stifling laughter.

They were starting to load us into the back of a squad car when one more car entered the level. It stopped next to us and a policeman wearing a fancy uniform jumped out of the vehicle. "Hold on," shouted the new arrival. "Release those two. Take those handcuffs off and let me talk to them. They are special forces and were operating undercover."

"Yes, Chief."

The men immediately followed the orders and Riley and I were led off to a position away from the others. The Police Chief reached into the bag he was carrying and pulled out a couple of cans of Mountain Dew. "Here you go, boys. You've earned this. I'll take care of everything on this end."

"So, we can go back to the car and go home?" I asked.

"No. I am afraid the car has been impounded." The Police Chief turned to me. "Your father has been contacted and will be here to pick you up shortly."

"What?" I shouted. "I'm a dead man. He's going to be so mad. It's going to be worse than the time I put the wrong kind of gas in the lawn mower."

"What's going on?" asked Riley. "Why do my legs hurt so bad."

The Chief looked at me. "It's up to you if you want to explain everything to him. I must return to my ship and begin searching for Amex. I will remain in control of this body until you are on your way home."

He began to turn away but stopped suddenly. He

reached into Riley's pocket, pulled out the small plastic-looking gun, and handed it to me. Riley just stared at us the whole time.

"Here," said the Chief, "You can keep this as a memento of our mission together."

I said, "You're giving a kid an advanced weapon? Maybe you guys aren't as smart as you think."

"Do not worry. That weapon is harmless to humans."

Without another word to us, he went and talked to the gathered police officers. Soon one of them came over and escorted us to one of the police cars. We sat inside for about twenty minutes. That's when my dad came to pick us up.

I started to try and give some sort of explanation to Dad, but it only took one look at the expression on his face for me to figure out that it was best if I kept my mouth shut. I've never seen anyone's that shade of red before.

During the drive home, no one spoke a word. Dad was too angry. I was too scared. Riley was too confused.

After we dropped Riley off at his house, we drove straight home and Dad pulled the car into the garage.

"Go to bed," grunted Dad. "We will talk about this in the morning."

I started to apologize but he cut me off.

"Go to bed."

I climbed out of the car and was almost through the open garage door when my father called to me from behind.

"Stop, human child," he shouted.

I turned to see him standing next to the car, the hammer that usually sat on the workbench in his hand.

I should have turned and run away, but I was too scared. That wasn't my dad, it was Amex.

"You are going to pay for ruining my plans. I will destroy your planet but not before I make you suffer for your interference." He moved toward me, raising the hammer as he did so.

Suddenly a pink blur shot past me. I watched in

shock as my mother slammed into Amex, driving him into the rear of the car. With one fluid motion, my mother, the woman who screams and climbs on a chair every time she sees a spider, somersaulted my dad's shoulders and got behind him. Instantly, she put him into the same sleeper hold that Riley had used on the policeman earlier.

My dad, Amex, slumped to the ground.

"Hurry," said my mom, "give me the weapon."

I fumbled in my pocket for a second and produced the small pistol. Mom grabbed the gun from my hand and aimed it at my dad's unconscious body. A small beam shot forth touching my father's head. The beam then retreated back into the gun. Mom twisted the pistol's handle, revealing a small control panel. She pushed a button and the gun hovered in the air. It floated out the garage door and up into the night sky.

Mom turned to me and smiled. "Now my mission is complete. I . . . we have captured Amex. We will be able to retrieve him once the containment weapon leaves your planet's atmosphere."

Realization hit me like one of Tommy Gruntman's dodgeball shots. "Hey, you knew Amex was going to do this all along. You set me up. That's why you let me keep the gun."

"There was a high probability that Amex would behave in this manner. It seemed like a risk worth taking."

"For you."

Mom smiled. "Thank you for your service to the galaxy and your planet."

"What do we do now?" I asked.

She reached down and grabbed Dad under the armpits and began to lift him from the ground. "I will need your help to carry him into the house. He is quite heavy and your mother does not drink enough Mountain Dew to do this by herself."

I grabbed Dad's legs and together we started carrying him toward the front door.

"What's going to happen to my mom and dad? Are they going to remember any of this?"

"Your mother will not have any recollection. I occupied her body while she was sleeping and I will return her to the bed when I transfer out."

"What about Dad? How much will he remember? Will he forget about me stealing the car and getting stopped by the police?"

"I'm afraid not," said Mom. "He will remember everything except for the few minutes when Amex inhabited his body."

"Isn't there anything you can do? Can't you wipe his memory or something?"

"I'm afraid not. But you can be proud of what you have done and you have the gratitude of the entire galaxy."

I shook my head. "A lot of good that's going to do me."

Who?

Veronica Leigh has been published in numerous anthologies, journals, and magazines. She aspires to be the Jane Austen of her generation and she makes her home in Indiana.

Randall Andrews says: I am the author of two books, one of which won the National Indie Excellence Award for best fantasy novel. My short stories have been nominated for a Locus Award, won the Write Michigan Short Story Contest, and been included in the anthology *The Best of Abyss & Apex: Vol. 3*. My poetry has appeared in places like *Illumen, Dreams & Nightmares, Space & Time, Abyss & Apex,* and *Star*Line*.

Maureen Mancini Amaturo, New York-based fashion/beauty writer with an MFA in Creative Writing, teaches writing, leads the Sound Shore Writers Group, which she founded in 2007, and produces literary and gallery events. Her fiction, essays, creative non-fiction, poetry, and comedy, are widely published appearing in: Half Hour To Kill, Paper Dragon, The Dark Sire, Every Day Fiction, Coffin Bell Journal, Drunken Pen, Flash Non-Fiction Food

Anthology (Woodhall Press,) Things That Go Bump (Sez Publishing,) Film Noir Before It Was Cool (Weasel Press), The Year Anthology (Crack The Spine,) Little Old Lady Comedy, Points In Case, and others. Once named "America's next Flannery O' Connor," Maureen was nominated for The Bram Stoker Award and the TDS Creative Fiction Award and was awarded Honorable Mention and Certificate of Excellence in poetry from Havik Literary Journal. Her poem, "Edgar Allan Poe and the Telemarketer" was a winner in Academy of the Heart and Mind 13 Halloween Tales Contest. A handwriting analyst diagnosed her with an overdeveloped imagination. She's working to live up to that.

James Rumpel is a retired high school math teacher who has decided to spend part of his new found free time trying to turn some of the many odd ideas circling his brain into stories. He lives in Wisconsin with his wonderful wife, Mary.

www.ingramcontent.com/pod-product-compliance
Lightning Source LLC
LaVergne TN
LVHW012031060526
838201LV00061B/4553